CINDERELLA
And Other Stories

CINDERELLA
And Other Stories

RICHARD HARDING DAVIS

WILDSIDE PRESS

CINDERELLA AND OTHER STORES

This edition published 2005 by Wildside Press, LLC.
www.wildsidepress.com

CONTENTS

Cinderella 7

Miss Delamar's Understudy 26

The Editor's Story 48

An Assisted Emigrant 64

The Reporter Who Made Himself King 72

CINDERELLA

The servants of the Hotel Salisbury, which is so called because it is situated on Broadway and conducted on the American plan by a man named Riggs, had agreed upon a date for their annual ball and volunteer concert, and had announced that it would eclipse every other annual ball in the history of the hotel. As the Hotel Salisbury had been only two years in existence, this was not an idle boast, and it had the effect of inducing many people to buy the tickets, which sold at a dollar apiece, and were good for "one gent and a lady," and entitled the bearer to a hat-check without extra charge.

In the flutter of preparation all ranks were temporarily levelled, and social barriers taken down with the mutual consent of those separated by them; the night-clerk so far unbent as to personally request the colored hall-boy Number Eight to play a banjo solo at the concert, which was to fill in the pauses between the dances, and the chambermaids timidly consulted with the lady telegraph operator and the lady in charge of the telephone, as to whether or not they intended to wear hats.

And so every employee on every floor of the hotel was working individually for the success of the ball, from the engineers in charge of the electric light plant in the cellar, to the night-watchman on the ninth story, and the elevator-boys who belonged to no floor in particular.

Miss Celestine Terrell, who was Mrs. Grahame West in private life, and young Grahame West, who played the part opposite to hers in the Gilbert and Sullivan Opera that was then in the third month of its New York run, were among the honored patrons of the Hotel Salisbury. Miss Terrell, in her utter inability to adjust the American coinage to English standards, and also in the kindness of her heart, had given too generous tips to all of the hotel waiters, and some of this money had passed into the gallery window of the

Broadway Theatre, where the hotel waiters had heard her sing and seen her dance, and had failed to recognize her young husband in the Lord Chancellor's wig and black silk court dress. So they knew that she was a celebrated personage, and they urged the *maître d'hôtel* to invite her to the ball, and then persuade her to take a part in their volunteer concert.

Paul, the head-waiter, or "Pierrot," as Grahame West called him, because it was shorter, as he explained, hovered over the two young English people one night at supper, and served them lavishly with his own hands.

"Miss Terrell," said Paul, nervously—"I beg pardon, Madam, Mrs. Grahame West, I should say—I would like to make an invitation to you."

Celestine looked at her husband inquiringly, and bowed her head for Paul to continue.

"The employees of the Salisbury give the annual ball and concert on the sixteenth of December, and the committee have inquired and requested of me, on account of your kindness, to ask you would you be so polite as to sing a little song for us at the night of our ball?"

The head-waiter drew a long breath and straightened himself with a sense of relief at having done his part, whether the Grahame Wests did theirs or not.

As a rule, Miss Terrell did not sing in private, and had only broken this rule twice, when the inducements which led her to do so were forty pounds for each performance, and the fact that her beloved Princess of Wales was to be present. So she hesitated for an instant.

"Why, you are very good," she said, doubtfully. "Will there be any other people there—any one not an employee, I mean?"

Paul misunderstood her and became a servant again.

"No, I am afraid there will be only the employees, Madam," he said.

"Oh, then, I should be very glad to come," murmured Celestine, sweetly. "But I never sing out of the theatre, so you mustn't mind if it is not good."

The head-waiter played a violent tattoo on the back of the chair in his delight, and balanced and bowed.

"Ah, we are very proud and pleased that we can induce Madam to make so great exceptions," he declared. "The committee will be most happy. We will send a carriage for Madam, and a bouquet for Madam also," he added grandly, as one who was not to be denied the etiquette to which he plainly showed he was used.

"Will we come?" cried Van Bibber, incredulously, as he and Travers sat watching Grahame make up in his dressing-room. "I should say we would come. And you must all take supper with us first, and we will get Letty Chamberlain from the Gaiety Company and Lester to come too, and make them each do a turn."

"And we can dance on the floor ourselves, can't we?" asked Grahame West, "as they do at home Christmas-eve in the servants' hall, when her ladyship dances in the same set with the butler and the men waltz with the cook."

"Well, over here," said Van Bibber, "you'll have to be careful that you're properly presented to the cook first, or she'll appeal to the floor committee and have you thrown out."

"The interesting thing about that ball," said Travers, as he and Van Bibber walked home that night, "is the fact that those hotel people are getting a galaxy of stars to amuse them for nothing who wouldn't exhibit themselves at a Fifth Avenue dance for all the money in Wall Street. And the joke of it is going to be that the servants will vastly prefer the banjo solo by hall-boy Number Eight."

Lyric Hall lies just this side of the Forty-second Street station along the line of the Sixth Avenue Elevated road, and you can look into its windows from the passing train. It was after one o'clock when the invited guests and their friends pushed open the storm-doors and were recognized by the anxious committee-men who were taking tickets at the top of the stairs. The committee-men fled in different directions, shouting for Mr. Paul, and Mr. Paul arrived beaming with delight and moisture, and presented a huge bouquet to Mrs. West, and welcomed her friends with hospitable warmth.

Mrs. West and Miss Chamberlain took off their hats and the men gave up their coats, not without misgivings, to a sleepy young man who said pleasantly, as he dragged them into the coat-room window, "that they would be playing in great luck if they ever saw them again."

"I don't need to give you no checks," he explained: "just ask for the coats with real fur on 'em. Nobody else has any."

There was a balcony overhanging the floor, and the invited guests were escorted to it, and given seats where they could look down upon the dancers below, and the committee-men, in dangling badges with edges of silver fringe, stood behind their chairs and poured out champagne for them lavishly, and tore up the wine-check which the barkeeper brought with it, with princely hospitality.

The entrance of the invited guests created but small interest, and neither the beauty of the two English girls nor Lester's well-known features, which smiled from shop-windows and on every ash-barrel in the New York streets, aroused any particular comment. The employees were much more occupied with the Lancers then in progress, and with the joyful actions of one of their number who was playing blindman's-bluff with himself, and swaying from set to set in search of his partner, who had given him up as hopeless and retired to the supper-room for crackers and beer.

Some of the ladies wore bonnets, and others wore flowers in their hair, and a half-dozen were in gowns which were obviously intended for dancing and nothing else. But none of them were in *décolleté* gowns. A few wore gloves. They had copied the fashions of their richer sisters with the intuitive taste of the American girl of their class, and they waltzed quite as well as the ladies whose dresses they copied, and many of them were exceedingly pretty. The costumes of the gentlemen varied from the clothes they wore nightly when waiting on the table, to cutaway coats with white satin ties, and the regular blue and brass-buttoned uniform of the hotel.

"I am going to dance," said Van Bibber, "if Mr. Pierrot will present me to one of the ladies."

Paul introduced him to a lady in a white cheese-cloth dress and black walking-shoes, with whom no one else would dance, and the musicians struck up "The Band Played On," and they launched out upon a slippery floor.

Van Bibber was conscious that his friends were applauding him in dumb show from the balcony, and when his partner asked who they were, he repudiated them altogether, and said he could not imagine, but that he guessed from their bad manners they were professional entertainers hired for the evening.

The music stopped abruptly, and as he saw Mrs. West leaving the balcony, he knew that his turn had come, and as she passed him he applauded her vociferously, and as no one else applauded even slightly, she grew very red.

Her friends knew that they formed the audience which she dreaded, and she knew that they were rejoicing in her embarrassment, which the head of the downstairs department, as Mr. Paul described him, increased to an hysterical point by introducing her as "Miss Ellen Terry, the great English actress, who would now oblige with a song."

The man had seen the name of the wonderful English actress on the billboards in front of Abbey's Theatre, and he had been told that Miss Terrell was English, and confused the two names. As he passed Van Bibber he drew his waistcoat into shape with a proud shrug of his shoulders, and said, anxiously, "I gave your friend a good introduction, anyway, didn't I?"

"You did, indeed," Van Bibber answered. "You couldn't have surprised her more; and it made a great hit with me, too."

No one in the room listened to the singing. The gentlemen had crossed their legs comfortably and were expressing their regret to their partners that so much time was wasted in sandwiching songs between the waltzes, and the ladies were engaged in criticizing Celestine's hair, which she wore in a bun. They thought that it might be English, but it certainly was not their idea of good style.

Celestine was conscious of the fact that her husband and Lester were hanging far over the balcony, holding their hands to their eyes as though they were opera-glasses, and exclaiming with admiration and delight; and when she had finished the first verse, they pretended to think that the song was over, and shouted, "Bravo, encore," and applauded frantically, and then apparently overcome with confusion at their mistake, sank back entirely from sight.

"I think Miss Terrell's an elegant singer," Van Bibber's partner said to him. "I seen her at the hotel frequently. She has such a pleasant way with her, quite ladylike. She's the only actress I ever saw that has retained her timidity. She acts as though she were shy, don't she?"

Van Bibber, who had spent a month on the Thames the summer before, with the Grahame Wests, surveyed Celestine with sudden interest, as though he had never seen her before until that moment, and agreed that she did look shy, one might almost say frightened to death. Mrs. West rushed through the second verse of the song, bowed breathlessly, and ran down the steps of the stage and back to the refuge of the balcony, while the audience applauded with perfunctory politeness and called clamorously to the musicians to "Let her go!"

"And that is the song," commented Van Bibber, "that gets six encores and three calls every night on Broadway!"

Grahame West affected to be greatly chagrined at his wife's failure to charm the chambermaids and porters with her little love-song, and when his turn came, he left them with alacrity, assuring them that they would now see the difference, as he would sing a song better suited to their level.

But the song that had charmed London and captured the unprotected coast town of New York, fell on heedless ears; and except the evil ones in the gallery, no one laughed and no one listened, and Lester declared with tears in his eyes that he would not go through such an ordeal for the receipts of an Actors' Fund Benefit.

Van Bibber's partner caught him laughing at Grahame West's vain efforts to amuse, and said, tolerantly, that Mr. West was certainly comical, but that she had a lady friend with her who could recite pieces which were that comic that you'd die of laughing. She presented her friend to Van Bibber, and he said he hoped that they were going to hear her recite, as laughing must be a pleasant death. But the young lady explained that she had had the misfortune to lose her only brother that summer, and that she had given up everything but dancing in consequence. She said she did not think it looked right to see a girl in mourning recite comic monologues.

Van Bibber struggled to be sympathetic, and asked what her brother had died of? She told him that "he died of a Thursday," and the conversation came to an embarrassing pause.

Van Bibber's partner had another friend in a gray corduroy waistcoat and tan shoes, who was of Hebraic appearance. He also wore several very fine rings, and officiated with what was certainly religious tolerance at the M.E. Bethel Church. She said he was an elegant or—gan—ist, putting the emphasis on the second syllable, which made Van Bibber think that she was speaking of some religious body to which he belonged. But the organist made his profession clear by explaining that the committee had just invited him to oblige the company with a solo on the piano, but that he had been hitting the champagne so hard that he doubted if he could tell the keys from the pedals, and he added that if they'd excuse him he would go to sleep, which he immediately did with his head on the shoulder of the lady recitationist, who tactfully tried not to notice that he was there.

They were all waltzing again, and as Van Bibber guided his partner for a second time around the room, he noticed a particularly handsome girl in a walking-dress, who was doing some sort of a fancy step with a solemn, grave-faced young man in the hotel livery. They seemed by their manner to know each other very well, and they had apparently practised the step that they were doing often before.

The girl was much taller than the man, and was superior to him in every way. Her movements were freer and less conscious, and she carried her head and shoulders as though she had never bent them above a broom. Her complexion was soft and her hair of the finest, deepest auburn. Among all the girls upon the floor she was the most remarkable, even if her dancing had not immediately distinguished her.

The step which she and her partner were exhibiting was one that probably had been taught her by a professor of dancing at some East Side academy, at the rate of fifty cents per hour, and which she no doubt believed was the latest step danced in the gilded halls of the Few Hundred. In this waltz the two dancers held each other's hands, and the man swung his partner behind him, and then would turn and take up the step with her where they had dropped it; or they swung around and around each other several times, as people do in fancy skating, and sometimes he spun her so quickly one way that the skirt of her walking-dress was wound as tightly around her legs and ankles as a cord around a top, and then as he swung her in the opposite direction, it unwound again, and wrapped about her from the other side. They varied this when it pleased them with balancings and steps and posturings that were not sufficiently extravagant to bring any comment from the other dancers, but which were so full of grace and feeling for time and rhythm, that Van Bibber continually reversed his partner so that he might not for an instant lose sight of the girl with auburn hair.

"She is a very remarkable dancer," he said at last, apologetically.

"Do you know who she is?"

His partner had observed his interest with increasing disapproval, and she smiled triumphantly now at the chance that his question gave her.

"She is the seventh floor chambermaid," she said. "I," she added in a tone which marked the social superiority, "am a checker and marker."

"Really?" said Van Bibber, with a polite accent of proper awe.

He decided that he must see more of this Cinderella of the Hotel Salisbury; and dropping his partner by the side of the lady recitationist, he bowed his thanks and hurried to the gallery for a better view.

When he reached it he found his professional friends hanging over the railing, watching every movement which the girl made with an intense and unaffected interest.

"Have you noticed that girl with red hair?" he asked, as he pulled up a chair beside them.

But they only nodded and kept their eyes fastened on the opening in the crowd through which she had disappeared.

"There she is," Grahame West cried excitedly, as the girl swept out from the mass of dancers into the clear space. "Now you can see what I mean, Celestine," he said. "Where he turns her like that. We could do it in the shadow-dance in the second act. It's very pretty. She lets go his right hand and then he swings her and balances backward until she takes up the step again, when she faces him. It is very simple and very effective. Isn't it, George?"

Lester nodded and said, "Yes, very. She's a born dancer. You can teach people steps, but you can't teach them to be graceful."

"She reminds me of Sylvia Grey," said Miss Chamberlain. "There's nothing violent about it, or faked, is there? It's just the poetry of motion, without any tricks."

Lester, who was a trick dancer himself, and Grahame West, who was one of the best eccentric dancers in England, assented to this cheerfully.

Van Bibber listened to the comments of the authorities and smiled grimly. The contrast which their lives presented to that of the young girl whom they praised so highly, struck him as being most interesting. Here were two men who had made comic dances a profound and serious study, and the two women who had lifted dancing to the plane of a fine art, all envying and complimenting a girl who was doing for her own pleasure that which was to them hard work and a livelihood. But while they were going back the next day to be applauded and petted and praised by a friendly public, she was to fly like Cinderella, to take up her sweeping and dusting and the making of beds, and the answering of peremptory summonses from electric buttons.

"A good teacher could make her worth one hundred dollars a week in six lessons," said Lester, dispassionately. "I'd be willing to make her an offer myself, if I hadn't too many dancers in the piece already."

"A hundred dollars—that's twenty pounds," said Mrs. Grahame West. "You do pay such prices over here! But I quite agree that she is very graceful; and she is so unconscious, too, isn't she?"

The interest in Cinderella ceased when the waltzing stopped, and the attention of those in the gallery was riveted with equal intensity upon Miss Chamberlain and Travers who had faced each other in a quadrille, Miss Chamberlain having accepted the assistant barkeeper for a partner, while Travers contented himself with a tall, elderly female, who in business hours had entire charge of the linen department. The barkeeper was a melancholy man with a dyed mustache, and when he asked the English dancer from what hotel she came, and she, thinking he meant at what hotel was she stopping, told him, he said that that was a slow place, and that if she would let him know when she had her night off, he would be pleased to meet her at the Twenty-third station of the Sixth Avenue road on the uptown side, and would take her to the theatre, for which, he explained, he was able to obtain tickets for nothing, as so many men gave him their return checks for drinks.

Miss Chamberlain told him in return, that she just doted on the theatre, and promised to meet him the very next evening. She sent him anonymously instead two seats in the front row for her performance. She had much delight the next night in watching his countenance when, after arriving somewhat late and cross, he recognized the radiant beauty on the stage as the young person with whom he had condescended to dance.

When the quadrille was over she introduced him to Travers, and Travers told him he mixed drinks at the Knickerbocker Club, and that his greatest work was a Van Bibber cocktail. And when the barkeeper asked for the recipe and promised to "push it along," Travers told him he never made it twice the same, as it depended entirely on his mood.

Mrs. Grahame West and Lester were scandalized at the conduct of these two young people and ordered the party home, and as the dance was growing somewhat noisy and the gentlemen were smoking as they danced, the invited guests made their bows to Mr. Paul and went out into cold, silent streets, followed by the thanks and compliments of seven bare-headed and swaying committeemen.

The next week Lester went on the road with his comic opera company; the Grahame Wests sailed to England, Letty Chamberlain and the other "Gee Gees," as Travers called the Gayety Girls, departed for Chicago, and Travers and Van Bibber were left alone.

The annual ball was a month in the past, when Van Bibber found Travers at breakfast at their club, and dropped into a chair beside him with a sigh of weariness and indecision.

"What's the trouble? Have some breakfast?" said Travers, cheerfully.

"Thank you, no," said Van Bibber, gazing at his friend doubtfully; "I want to ask you what you think of this. Do you remember that girl at that servants' ball?"

"Which girl?—Tall girl with red hair—did fancy dance? Yes—why?"

"Well, I've been thinking about her lately," said Van Bibber, "and what they said of her dancing. It seems to me that if it's as good as they thought it was, the girl ought to be told of it and encouraged. They evidently meant what they said. It wasn't as though they were talking about her to her relatives and had to say something pleasant. Lester thought she could make a hundred dollars a week if she had had six lessons. Well, six lessons wouldn't cost much, not more than ten dollars at the most, and a hundred a week for an original outlay of ten is a good investment."

Travers nodded his head in assent, and whacked an egg viciously with his spoon. "What's your scheme?" he said. "Is your idea to help the lady for her own sake—sort of a philanthropic snap—or as a speculation? We might make it pay as a speculation. You see nobody knows about her except you and me. We might form her into a sort of stock company and teach her to dance, and secure her engagements and then take our commission out of her salary. Is that what you were thinking of doing?"

"No, that was not my idea," said Van Bibber, smiling. "I hadn't any plan. I just thought I'd go down to that hotel and tell her that in the opinion of the four people best qualified to know what good dancing is, she is a good dancer, and then leave the rest to her. She must have some friends or relations who would help her to take a start. If it's true that she can make a hit as a dancer, it seems a pity that she shouldn't know it, doesn't it? If she succeeded, she'd make a pot of money, and if she failed she'd be just where she is now."

Travers considered this subject deeply, with knit brows.

"That's so," he said. "I'll tell you what let's do. Let's go see some of the managers of those continuous performance places, and tell them we have a dark horse that the Grahame Wests and Letty Chamberlain herself and George Lester think is the coming dancer of the age, and ask them to give her a chance. And we'll make some sort of a contract with them. We ought to fix it so that she is to get bigger money the longer they keep her in the bill, have her salary on a rising scale. Come on," he exclaimed, warming to the idea. "Let's go now. What have you got to do?"

"I've got nothing better to do than just that," Van Bibber declared, briskly.

The managers whom they interviewed were interested but noncommittal. They agreed that the girl must be a remarkable dancer indeed to warrant such praise from such authorities, but they wanted to see her and judge for themselves, and they asked to be given her address, which the impresarios refused to disclose. But they secured from the managers the names of several men who taught fancy dancing, and who prepared aspirants for the vaudeville stage, and having obtained from them their prices and their opinion as to how long a time would be required to give the finishing touches to a dancer already accomplished in the art, they directed their steps to the Hotel Salisbury.

"'From the Seventh Story to the Stage,'" said Travers. "She will make very good newspaper paragraphs, won't she? 'The New American Dancer, endorsed by Celestine Terrell, Letty Chamberlain, and Cortlandt Van Bibber.' And we could get her outside engagements to dance at studios and evening parties after her regular performance, couldn't we?" he continued. "She ought to ask from fifty to a hundred dollars a night. With her regular salary that would average about three hundred and fifty a week. She is probably making three dollars a week now, and eats in the servants' hall."

"And then we will send her abroad," interrupted Van Bibber, taking up the tale, "and she will do the music halls in London. If she plays three halls a night, say one on the Surrey Side, and Islington, and a smart West End hall like the Empire or the Alhambra, at fifteen guineas a turn, that would bring her in five hundred and twenty-five dollars a week. And then she would go to the Folies Bergère in Paris, and finally to Petersburg and Milan, and then come back to dance in the Grand Opera season, under Gus Harris, with a great international reputation, and hung with flowers and medals and diamond sunbursts and things."

"Rather," said Travers, shaking his head enthusiastically. "And after that we must invent a new dance for her, with colored lights and mechanical snaps and things, and have it patented; and finally she will get her picture on soda-cracker boxes and cigarette advertisements, and have a race-horse named after her, and give testimonials for nerve tonics and soap. Does fame reach farther than that?"

"I think not," said Van Bibber, "unless they give her name to a new make of bicycle. We must give her a new name, anyway, and rechristen her, whatever her name may be. We'll call her Cinderella—La Cinderella. That sounds fine, doesn't it, even if it is rather long for the very largest type."

"It isn't much longer than Carmencita," suggested the other. "And people who have the proud knowledge of knowing her like you and me will call her 'Cinders' for short. And when we read of her dancing before the Czar of All the Russias, and leading the ballet at the Grand Opera House in Paris, we'll say, 'that is our handiwork,' and we will feel that we have not lived in vain."

"Seventh floor, please," said Van Bibber to the elevator boy.

The elevator boy was a young man of serious demeanor, with a smooth-shaven face and a square, determined jaw. There was something about him which seemed familiar, but Van Bibber could not determine just what it was. The elevator stopped to allow some people to leave it at the second floor, and as the young man shoved the door to again, Van Bibber asked him if he happened to know of a chambermaid with red hair, a tall girl on the seventh floor, a girl who danced very well.

The wire rope of the elevator slipped less rapidly through the hands of the young man who controlled it, and he turned and fixed his eyes with sudden interest on Van Bibber's face, and scrutinized him and his companion with serious consideration.

"Yes, I know her—I know who you mean, anyway," he said. "Why?"

"Why?" echoed Van Bibber, raising his eyes. "We wish to see her on a matter of business. Can you tell me her name?"

The elevator was running so slowly now that its movement upward was barely perceptible.

"Her name's Annie—Annie Crehan. Excuse me," said the young man, doubtfully, "ain't you the young fellows who came to our ball with that English lady, the one that sung?"

"Yes," Van Bibber assented, pleasantly. "We were there. That's where I've seen you before. You were there too, weren't you?"

"Me and Annie was dancing together most all the evening. I seen all youse watching her."

"Of course," exclaimed Van Bibber. "I remember you now. Oh, then you must know her quite well. Maybe you can help us. We want to put her on the stage."

The elevator came to a stop with an abrupt jerk, and the young man shoved his hands behind him, and leaned back against one of the mirrors in its side.

"On the stage," he repeated. "Why?"

Van Bibber smiled and shrugged his shoulders in some embarrassment at this peremptory challenge. But there was nothing in the young man's tone or manner that could give offence. He seemed much in earnest, and spoke as though they must understand that he had some right to question.

"Why? Because of her dancing. She is a very remarkable dancer. All of those actors with us that night said so. You must know that yourself better than any one else, since you can dance with her. She could make quite a fortune as a dancer, and we have persuaded several managers to promise to give her a trial. And if she needs money to pay for lessons, or to buy the proper dresses and slippers and things, we are willing to give it to her, or to lend it to her, if she would like that better."

"Why?" repeated the young man, immovably. His manner was not encouraging.

"Why—what?" interrupted Travers, with growing impatience.

"Why are you willing to give her money? You don't know her."

Van Bibber looked at Travers, and Travers smiled in some annoyance. The electric bell rang violently from different floors, but the young man did not heed it. He had halted the elevator between two landings, and he now seated himself on the velvet cushions and crossed one leg over the other, as though for a protracted debate. Travers gazed about him in humorous apprehension, as though alarmed at the position in which he found himself, hung as it were between the earth and sky.

"I swear I am an unarmed man," he said, in a whisper.

"Our intentions are well meant, I assure you," said Van Bibber, with an amused smile. "The girl is working ten hours a day for very little money, isn't she? You know she is, when she could make a great deal of money by working half as hard. We have some influence with theatrical people, and we meant merely to put her in the way of bettering her position, and to give her the chance to do something which she can do better than many others, while almost any one, I take it, can sweep and make beds. If she were properly managed, she could become a great dancer, and delight thousands of people—add to the gayety of nations, as it were. She's hardly doing that now, is she? Have you any objections to that? What right have you to make objections, anyway?"

The young man regarded the two young gentlemen before him with a dogged countenance, but there was now in his eyes a look of helplessness and of great disquietude.

"We're engaged to be married, Annie and me," he said. "That's it."

"Oh," exclaimed Van Bibber, "I beg your pardon. That's different. Well, in that case, you can help us very much, if you wish. We leave it entirely with you!"

"I don't want that you should leave it with me," said the young man, harshly. "I don't want to have nothing to do with it. Annie can speak for herself. I knew it was coming to this," he said, leaning forward and clasping his hands together, "or something like this. I've never felt dead sure of Annie, never once. I always knew something would happen."

"Why, nothing has happened," said Van Bibber, soothingly. "You would both benefit by it. We would be as willing to help two as one. You would both be better off."

The young man raised his head and stared at Van Bibber reprovingly.

"You know better than that," he said. "You know what I'd look like. Of course she could make money as a dancer, I've known that for some time, but she hasn't thought of it yet, and she'd never have thought of it herself. But the question isn't me or what I want. It's Annie. Is she going to be happier or not, that's the question. And I'm telling you that she couldn't be any happier than she is now. I know that, too. We're just as contented as two folks ever was. We've been saving for three months, and buying furniture from the instalment people, and next month we were going to move into a flat on Seventh Avenue, quite handy to the hotel. If she goes onto the stage could she be any happier? And if you're honest in saying you're thinking of the two of us—I ask you where would I come in? I'll be pulling this wire rope and she'll be all over the country, and her friends won't be my friends and her ways won't be my ways. She'll get out of reach of me in a week, and I won't be in it. I'm not the sort to go loafing round while my wife supports me, carrying her satchel for her. And there's nothing I can do but just this. She'd come back here some day and live in the front floor suite, and I'd pull her up and down in this elevator.

That's what will happen. Here's what you two gentlemen are doing." The young man leaned forward eagerly. "You're offering a change to two people that are as well off now as they ever hope to be, and they're contented. We don't know nothin' better. Now, are you dead sure that you're giving us something better than what we've got? You can't make me any happier than I am, and as far as Annie knows, up to now, she couldn't be better fixed, and no one could care for her more.

"My God! gentlemen," he cried, desperately, "think! She's all I've got. There's lots of dancers, but she's not a dancer to me, she's just Annie. I don't want her to delight the gayety of nations. I want her for myself. Maybe I'm selfish, but I can't help that. She's mine, and you're trying to take her away from me. Suppose she was your girl, and some one was sneaking her away from you. You'd try to stop it, wouldn't you, if she was all you had?" He stopped breathlessly and stared alternately from one to the other of the young men before him. Their countenances showed an expression of well-bred concern.

"It's for you to judge," he went on, helplessly; "if you want to take the responsibility, well and good, that's for you to say. I'm not stopping you, but she's all I've got."

The young man stopped, and there was a pause while he eyed them eagerly. The elevator bell rang out again with vicious indignation.

Travers struck at the toe of his boot with his stick and straightened his shoulders.

"I think you're extremely selfish, if you ask me," he said.

The young man stood up quickly and took his elevator rope in both hands. "All right," he said, quietly, "that settles it. I'll take you up to Annie now, and you can arrange it with her. I'm not standing in her way."

"Hold on," protested Van Bibber and Travers in a breath. "Don't be in such a hurry," growled Travers.

The young man stood immovable, with his hands on the wire and looking down on them, his face full of doubt and distress.

"I don't want to stand in Annie's way," he repeated, as though to himself. "I'll do whatever you say. I'll take you to the seventh floor or I'll drop you to the street. It's up to you, gentlemen," he added, helplessly, and turning his back to them threw his arm against the wall of the elevator and buried his face upon it.

There was an embarrassing pause, during which Van Bibber scowled at himself in the mirror opposite as though to ask it what a man who looked like that should do under such trying circumstances.

He turned at last and stared at Travers. "'Where ignorance is bliss, it's folly to be wise,'" he whispered, keeping his face toward his friend. "What do you say? Personally I don't see myself in the part of Providence. It's the case of the poor man and his one ewe lamb, isn't it?"

"We don't want his ewe lamb, do we?" growled Travers. "It's a case of the dog in a manger, I say. I thought we were going to be fairy godfathers to 'La Cinderella.'"

"The lady seems to be supplied with a most determined godfather as it is," returned Van Bibber.

The elevator boy raised his face and stared at them with haggard eyes.

"Well?" he begged.

Van Bibber smiled upon him reassuringly, with a look partly of respect and partly of pity.

"You can drop us to the street," he said.

MISS DELAMAR'S UNDERSTUDY

A young man runs two chances of marrying the wrong woman. He marries her because she is beautiful, and because he persuades himself that every other lovable attribute must be associated with such beauty, or because she is in love with him. If this latter is the case, she gives certain values to what he thinks and to what he says which no other woman gives, and so he observes to himself, "This is the woman who best understands *me*."

You can reverse this and say that young women run the same risks, but as men are seldom beautiful, the first danger is eliminated. Women still marry men, however, because they are loved by them, and in time the woman grows to depend upon this love and to need it, and is not content without it, and so she consents to marry the man for no other reason than because he cares for her. For if a dog, even, runs up to you wagging his tail and acting as though he were glad to see you, you pat him on the head and say, "What a nice dog." You like him because he likes you, and not because he belongs to a fine breed of animal and could take blue ribbons at bench shows.

This is the story of a young man who was in love with a beautiful woman, and who allowed her beauty to compensate him for many other things. When she failed to understand what he said to her he smiled and looked at her and forgave her at once, and when she began to grow uninteresting, he would take up his hat and go away, and so he never knew how very uninteresting she might possibly be if she were given time enough in which to demonstrate the fact. He never considered that, were he married to her, he could not take up his hat and go away when she became uninteresting, and that her remarks, which were not brilliant, could not be smiled away either. They would rise up and greet him every morning, and would be the last thing he would hear at night.

Miss Delamar's beauty was so conspicuous that to pretend not to notice it was more foolish than well-bred. You got along more easily and simply by accepting it at once, and referring to it, and enjoying its effect upon other people. To go out of one's way to talk of other things when every one, even Miss Delamar herself, knew what must be uppermost in your mind, always seemed as absurd as to strain a point in politeness, and to pretend not to notice that a guest had upset his claret, or any other embarrassing fact. For Miss Delamar's beauty was so distinctly embarrassing that this was the only way to meet it—to smile and pass it over and to try, if possible, to get on to something else. It was on account of this extraordinary quality in her appearance that every one considered her beauty as something which transcended her private ownership, and which belonged by right to the polite world at large, to any one who could appreciate it properly, just as though it were a sunset or a great work of art or of nature. And so, when she gave away her photographs no one thought it meant anything more serious than a recognition on her part of the fact that it would have been unkind and selfish in her not to have shared the enjoyment of so much loveliness with others.

Consequently, when she sent one of her largest and most aggravatingly beautiful photographs to young Stuart, it was no sign that she cared especially for him.

How much young Stuart cared for Miss Delamar, however, was an open question, and a condition yet to be discovered. That he cared for some one, and cared so much that his imagination had begun to picture the awful joys and responsibilities of marriage, was only too well known to himself, and was a state of mind already suspected by his friends.

Stuart was a member of the New York bar, and the distinguished law firm to which he belonged was very proud of its junior member, and treated him with indulgence and affection, which was not unmixed with amusement. For Stuart's legal knowledge had been gathered in many odd corners of the globe, and was various and peculiar. It had been his pleasure to study the laws by which men ruled other men in every condition of life, and under every sun. The regulations of a new mining camp were fraught with as great interest to him as the accumulated precedents of the English Constitution, and he had investigated the rulings of the mixed courts of Egypt and of the government of the little Dutch republic near the Cape with as keen an effort to comprehend, as he had shown in studying the laws of the American colonies and of the Commonwealth of Massachusetts.

But he was not always serious, and it sometimes happened that after he had arrived at some queer little island where the native prince and the English governor sat in judgment together, his interest in the intricacies of their laws would give way to the more absorbing occupation of chasing wild boar or shooting at tigers from the top of an elephant. And so he was not only regarded as an authority on many forms of government and of law, into which no one else had ever taken the trouble to look, but his books on big game were eagerly read and his articles in the magazines were earnestly discussed, whether they told of the divorce laws of Dakota, and the legal rights of widows in Cambodia, or the habits of the Mexican lion.

Stuart loved his work better than he knew, but how well he loved Miss Delamar neither he nor his friends could tell. She was the most beautiful and lovely creature that he had ever seen, and of that only was he certain.

Stuart was sitting in the club one day when the conversation turned to matrimony. He was among his own particular friends, the men before whom he could speak seriously or foolishly without fear of being misunderstood or of having what he said retold and spoiled in the telling. There was Seldon, the actor, and Rives who painted pictures, and young Sloane, who travelled for pleasure and adventure, and Weimer who stayed at home and wrote for the reviews. They were all bachelors, and very good friends, and jealously guarded their little circle from the intrusion of either men or women.

"Of course the chief objection to marriage," Stuart said—it was the very day in which the picture had been sent to his rooms—"is the old one that you can't tell anything about it until you are committed to it forever. It is a very silly thing to discuss even, because there is no way of bringing it about, but there really should be some sort of a preliminary trial. As the man says in the play, 'you wouldn't buy a watch without testing it first.' You don't buy a hat even without putting it on, and finding out whether it is becoming or not, or whether your peculiar style of ugliness can stand it. And yet men go gayly off and get married, and make the most awful promises, and alter their whole order of life and risk the happiness of some lovely creature on trust, as it were, knowing absolutely nothing of the new conditions and responsibilities of the life before them. Even a river pilot has to serve an apprenticeship before he gets a license, and yet we are allowed to take just as great risks, and only because we *want* to take them. It's awful, and it's all wrong."

"Well, I don't see what one is going to do about it," commented young Sloane, lightly, "except to get divorced. That road is always open."

Sloane was starting the next morning for the Somali Country, in Abyssinia, to shoot rhinoceros, and his interest in matrimony was in consequence somewhat slight.

"It isn't the fear of the responsibilities that keeps Stuart, nor any one of us back," said Weimer, contemptuously. "It's because we're selfish. That's the whole truth of the matter. We love our work, or our pleasure, or to knock about the world, better than we do any particular woman. When one of us comes to love the woman best, his conscience won't trouble him long about the responsibilities of marrying her."

"Not at all," said Stuart, "I am quite sincere; I maintain that there should be a preliminary stage. Of course there can't be, and it's absurd to think of it, but it would save a lot of unhappiness."

"Well," said Seldon, dryly, "when you've invented a way to prevent marriage from being a lottery, let me know, will you?" He stood up and smiled nervously. "Any of you coming to see us tonight?" he asked.

"That's so," exclaimed Weimer, "I forgot. It's the first night of 'A Fool and His Money,' isn't it? Of course we're coming."

"I told them to put a box away for you in case you wanted it," Seldon continued. "Don't expect much. It's a silly piece, and I've a silly part, and I'm very bad in it. You must come around to supper, and tell me where I'm bad in it, and we will talk it over. You coming, Stuart?"

"My dear old man," said Stuart, reproachfully. "Of course I am. I've had my seats for the last three weeks. Do you suppose I could miss hearing you mispronounce all the Hindostanee I've taught you?"

"Well, good-night then," said the actor, waving his hand to his friends as he moved away. "'We, who are about to die, salute you!'"

"Good luck to you," said Sloane, holding up his glass. "To the Fool and His Money," he laughed. He turned to the table again, and sounded the bell for the waiter. "Now let's send him a telegram and wish him success, and all sign it," he said, "and don't you fellows tell him that I wasn't in front tonight. I've got to go to a dinner the Travellers' Club are giving me." There was a protesting chorus of remonstrance. "Oh, I don't like it any better than you do," said Sloane, "but I'll get away early and join you before the play's over. No one in the Travellers' Club, you see, has ever travelled farther from New York than London or the Riviera, and so when a member starts for Abyssinia they give him a dinner, and he has to take himself very seriously indeed, and cry with Seldon, 'I who am about to die, salute you.' If that man there was any use," he added, interrupting himself and pointing with his glass at Stuart, "he'd pack up his things tonight and come with me."

"Oh, don't urge him," remonstrated Weimer, who had travelled all over the world in imagination, with the aid of globes and maps, but never had got any farther from home than Montreal. "We can't spare Stuart. He has to stop here and invent a preliminary marriage state, so that if he finds he doesn't like a girl, he can leave her before it is too late."

"You sail at seven, I believe, and from Hoboken, don't you?" asked Stuart undisturbed. "If you'll start at eleven from the New York side, I think I'll go with you, but I hate getting up early; and then you see—I know what dangers lurk in Abyssinia, but who could tell what might not happen to him in Hoboken?"

When Stuart returned to his room, he found a large package set upright in an armchair and enveloped by many wrappings; but the handwriting on the outside told him at once from whom it came and what it might be, and he pounced upon it eagerly and tore it from its covers. The photograph was a very large one, and the likeness to the original so admirable that the face seemed to smile and radiate with all the loveliness and beauty of Miss Delamar herself. Stuart beamed upon it with genuine surprise and pleasure, and exclaimed delightedly to himself. There was a living quality about the picture which made him almost speak to it, and thank Miss Delamar through it for the pleasure she had given him and the honor she had bestowed. He was proud, flattered, and triumphant, and while he walked about the room deciding where he would place it, and holding the picture respectfully before him, he smiled upon it with grateful satisfaction.

He decided against his dressing-table as being too intimate a place for it, and so carried the picture on from his bedroom to the dining-room beyond, where he set it among his silver on the sideboard. But so little of his time was spent in this room that he concluded he would derive but little pleasure from it there, and so bore it back again into his library, where there were many other photographs and portraits, and where to other eyes than his own it would be less conspicuous.

He tried it first in one place and then in another; but in each position the picture predominated and asserted itself so markedly, that Stuart gave up the idea of keeping it inconspicuous, and placed it prominently over the fireplace, where it reigned supreme above every other object in the room. It was not only the most conspicuous object there, but the living quality which it possessed in so marked a degree, and which was due to its naturalness of pose and the excellence of the likeness, made it permeate the place like a presence and with the individuality of a real person. Stuart observed this effect with amused interest, and noted also that the photographs of other women had become commonplace in comparison like lithographs in a shop window, and that the more masculine accessories of a bachelor's apartment had grown suddenly aggressive and out of keeping. The liquor case and the racks of arms and of barbarous weapons which he had collected with such pride seemed to have lost their former value and meaning, and he instinctively began to gather up the mass of books and maps and photographs and pipes and gloves which lay scattered upon the table, and to put them in their proper place, or to shove them out of sight altogether. "If I'm to live up to that picture," he thought, "I must see that George keeps this room in better order—and I must stop wandering round here in my bathrobe."

His mind continued on the picture while he was dressing, and he was so absorbed in it and in analyzing the effect it had had upon him, that his servant spoke twice before he heard him.

"No," he answered, "I shall not dine here tonight." Dining at home was with him a very simple affair, and a somewhat lonely one, and he avoided it almost nightly by indulging himself in a more expensive fashion.

But even as he spoke an idea came to Stuart which made him reconsider his determination, and which struck him as so amusing, that he stopped pulling at his tie and smiled delightedly at himself in the glass before him.

"Yes," he said, still smiling, "I will dine here tonight. Get me anything in a hurry. You need not wait now; go get the dinner up as soon as possible."

The effect which the photograph of Miss Delamar had upon him, and the transformation it had accomplished in his room, had been as great as would have marked the presence there of the girl herself. While considering this it had come to Stuart, like a flash of inspiration, that here was a way by which he could test the responsibilities and conditions of married life without compromising either himself, or the girl to whom he would suppose himself to be married.

"I will put that picture at the head of the table," he said, "and I will play that it is she herself, her own, beautiful, lovely self, and I will talk to her and exchange views with her, and make her answer me just as she would were we actually married and settled." He looked at his watch and found it was just seven o'clock. "I will begin now," he said, "and I will keep up the delusion until midnight. Tonight is the best time to try the experiment because the picture is new now, and its influence will be all the more real. In a few weeks it may have lost some of its freshness and reality and will have become one of the fixtures in the room."

Stuart decided that under these new conditions it would be more pleasant to dine at Delmonico's, and he was on the point of asking the Picture what she thought of it, when he remembered that while it had been possible for him to make a practice of dining at that place as a bachelor, he could not now afford so expensive a luxury, and he decided that he had better economize in that particular and go instead to one of the table d'hôte restaurants in the neighborhood. He regretted not having thought of this sooner, for he did not care to dine at a table d'hôte in evening dress, as in some places it rendered him conspicuous. So, sooner than have this happen he decided to dine at home, as he had originally intended when he first thought of attempting this experiment, and then conducted the picture into dinner and placed her in an armchair facing him, with the candles full upon the face.

"Now this is something like," he exclaimed, joyously. "I can't imagine anything better than this. Here we are all to ourselves with no one to bother us, with no chaperone, or chaperone's husband either, which is generally worse. Why is it, my dear," he asked gayly, in a tone that he considered affectionate and husbandly, "that the attractive chaperones are always handicapped by such stupid husbands, and vice versa?"

"If that is true," replied the Picture, or replied Stuart, rather, for the picture, "I cannot be a very attractive chaperone." Stuart bowed politely at this, and then considered the point it had raised as to whether he had, in assuming both characters, the right to pay himself compliments. He decided against himself in this particular instance, but agreed that he was not responsible for anything the Picture might say, so long as he sincerely and fairly tried to make it answer him as he thought the original would do under like circumstances. From what he knew of the original under other conditions, he decided that he could give a very close imitation of her point of view.

Stuart's interest in his dinner was so real that he found himself neglecting his wife, and he had to pull himself up to his duty with a sharp reproof. After smiling back at her for a moment or two until his servant had again left them alone, he asked her to tell him what she had been doing during the day.

"Oh, nothing very important," said the Picture. "I went shopping in the morning and—"

Stuart stopped himself and considered this last remark doubtfully. "Now, how do I know she would go shopping?" he asked himself. "People from Harlem and women who like bargain counters, and who eat chocolate meringue for lunch, and then stop in at a continuous performance, go shopping. It must be the comic paper sort of wives who go about matching shades and buying hooks and eyes. Yes, I must have made Miss Delamar's understudy misrepresent her. I beg your pardon, my dear," he said aloud to the Picture. "You did *not* go shopping this morning. You probably went to a woman's luncheon somewhere. Tell me about that."

"Oh, yes, I went to lunch with the Antwerps," said the Picture, "and they had that Russian woman there who is getting up subscriptions for the Siberian prisoners. It's rather fine of her because it exiles her from Russia. And she is a princess."

"That's nothing," Stuart interrupted, "they're all princesses when you see them on Broadway."

"I beg your pardon," said the Picture.

"It's of no consequence," said Stuart, apologetically, "it's a comic song. I forgot you didn't like comic songs. Well—go on."

"Oh, then I went to a tea, and then I stopped in to hear Madame Ruvier read a paper on the Ethics of Ibsen, and she—"

Stuart's voice had died away gradually, and he caught himself wondering whether he had told George to lay in a fresh supply of cigars. "I beg your pardon," he said, briskly, "I was listening, but I was just wondering whether I had any cigars left. You were saying that you had been at Madame Ruvier's, and—"

"I am afraid that you were not interested," said the Picture. "Never mind, it's my fault. Sometimes I think I ought to do things of more interest, so that I should have something to talk to you about when you come home."

Stuart wondered at what hour he would come home now that he was married. As a bachelor he had been in the habit of stopping on his way up town from the law office at the club, or to take tea at the houses of the different girls he liked. Of course he could not do that now as a married man. He would instead have to limit his calls to married women, as all the other married men of his acquaintance did. But at the moment he could not think of any attractive married women who would like his dropping in on them in such a familiar manner, and the other sort did not as yet appeal to him.

He seated himself in front of the coal-fire in the library, with the Picture in a chair close beside him, and as he puffed pleasantly on his cigar he thought how well this suited him, and how delightful it was to find content in so simple and continuing a pleasure. He could almost feel the pressure of his wife's hand as it lay in his own, as they sat in silent sympathy looking into the friendly glow of the fire.

There was a long pleasant pause.

"They're giving Sloane a dinner tonight at the 'Travellers'," Stuart said at last, "in honor of his going to Abyssinia."

Stuart pondered for some short time as to what sort of a reply Miss Delamar's understudy ought to make to this innocent remark. He recalled the fact that on numerous occasions the original had shown not only a lack of knowledge in far-away places, but what was more trying, a lack of interest as well. For the moment he could not see her robbed of her pretty environment and tramping through undiscovered countries at his side. So the Picture's reply, when it came, was strictly in keeping with several remarks which Miss Delamar herself had made to him in the past.

"Yes," said the Picture, politely, "and where is Abyssinia—in India, isn't it?"

"No, not exactly," corrected Stuart, mildly; "you pass it on your way to India, though, as you go through the Red Sea. Sloane is taking Winchesters with him and a double express and a 'five fifty.' He wants to test their penetration. I think myself that the express is the best, but he says Selous and Chanler think very highly of the Winchester. I don't know, I never shot a rhinoceros. The time I killed that elephant," he went on, pointing at two tusks that stood with some assegais in a corner, "I used an express, and I had to let go with both barrels. I suppose, though, if I'd needed a third shot I'd have wished it was a Winchester. He was charging the smoke, you see, and I couldn't get away because I'd caught my foot—but I told you about that, didn't I?" Stuart interrupted himself to ask politely.

"Yes," said the Picture, cheerfully, "I remember it very well; it was very foolish of you."

Stuart straightened himself with a slightly injured air and avoided the Picture's eye. He had been stopped midway in what was one of his favorite stories, and it took a brief space of time for him to recover himself, and to sink back again into the pleasant lethargy in which he had been basking.

"Still," he said, "I think the express is the better gun."

"Oh, is an 'express' a gun?" exclaimed the Picture, with sudden interest. "Of course, I might have known."

Stuart turned in his chair and surveyed the Picture in some surprise. "But, my dear girl," he remonstrated kindly, "why didn't you ask, if you didn't know what I was talking about. What did you suppose it was?"

"I didn't know," said the Picture, "I thought it was something to do with his luggage. Abyssinia sounds so far away," she explained, smiling sweetly. "You can't expect one to be interested in such queer places, can you?"

"No," Stuart answered, reluctantly, and looking steadily at the fire, "I suppose not. But you see, my dear," he said, "I'd have gone with him, if I hadn't married you, and so I am naturally interested in his outfit. They wanted me to make a comparative study of the little semi-independent states down there, and of how far the Italian government allows them to rule themselves. That's what I was to have done."

But the Picture hastened to reassure him. "Oh, you mustn't think," she exclaimed, quickly, "that I mean to keep you at home. I love to travel, too. I want you to go on exploring places just as you've always done, only now I will go with you. We might do the Cathedral towns, for instance."

"The what!" gasped Stuart, raising his head. "Oh, yes, of course," he added, hurriedly, sinking back into his chair with a slightly bewildered expression. "That would be very nice. Perhaps your mother would like to go too; it's not a dangerous expedition, is it? I *was* thinking of taking you on a trip through the South Seas—but I suppose the Cathedral towns are just as exciting. Or we might even penetrate as far into the interior as the English lakes and read Wordsworth and Coleridge as we go."

Miss Delamar's understudy observed him closely for a moment, but he made no sign, and so she turned her eyes again to the fire with a slightly troubled look. She had not a strong sense of humor, but she was very beautiful.

Stuart's conscience troubled him for the next few moments, and he endeavored to make up for his impatience of the moment before, by telling the Picture how particularly well she was looking.

"It seems almost selfish to keep it all to myself," he mused.

"You don't mean," inquired the Picture, with tender anxiety, "that you want any one else here, do you? I'm sure I could be content to spend every evening like this. I've had enough of going out and talking to people I don't care about. Two seasons," she added, with the superior air of one who has put away childish things, "was quite enough of it for me."

"Well, I never took it as seriously as that," said Stuart, "but, of course, I don't want any one else here to spoil our evening. It is perfect."

He assured himself that it *was* perfect, but he wondered what was the loyal thing for a married couple to do when the conversation came to a dead stop. And did the conversation come to a stop because they preferred to sit in silent sympathy and communion, or because they had nothing interesting to talk about? Stuart doubted if silence was the truest expression of the most perfect confidence and sympathy. He generally found when he was interested, that either he or his companion talked all the time. It was when he was bored that he sat silent. But it was probably different with married people. Possibly they thought of each other during these pauses, and of their own affairs and interests, and then he asked himself how many interests could one fairly retain with which the other had nothing to do?

"I suppose," thought Stuart, "that I had better compromise and read aloud. Should you like me to read aloud?" he asked, doubtfully.

The Picture brightened perceptibly at this, and said that she thought that would be charming. "We might make it quite instructive," she suggested, entering eagerly into the idea. "We ought to agree to read so many pages every night. Suppose we begin with Guizot's 'History of France.' I have always meant to read that, the illustrations look so interesting."

"Yes, we might do that," assented Stuart, doubtfully. "It is in six volumes, isn't it? Suppose now, instead," he suggested, with an impartial air, "we begin that tomorrow night, and go this evening to see Seldon's new play, 'The Fool and His Money.' It's not too late, and he has saved a box for us, and Weimer and Rives and Sloane will be there, and—"

The Picture's beautiful face settled for just an instant in an expression of disappointment. "Of course," she replied slowly, "if you wish it. But I thought you said," she went on with a sweet smile, "that this was perfect. Now you want to go out again. Isn't this better than a hot theatre? You might put up with it for one evening, don't you think?"

"Put up with it!" exclaimed Stuart, enthusiastically; "I could spend every evening so. It was only a suggestion. It wasn't that I wanted to go so much as that I thought Seldon might be a little hurt if I didn't. But I can tell him you were not feeling very well, and that we will come some other evening. He generally likes to have us there on the first night, that's all. But he'll understand."

"Oh," said the Picture, "if you put it in the light of a duty to your friend, of course we will go."

"Not at all," replied Stuart, heartily; "I will read something. I should really prefer it. How would you like something of Browning's?"

"Oh, I read all of Browning once," said the Picture, "I think I should like something new."

Stuart gasped at this, but said nothing, and began turning over the books on the centre table. He selected one of the monthly magazines, and choosing a story which neither of them had read, sat down comfortably in front of the fire, and finished it without interruption and to the satisfaction of the Picture and himself. The story had made the half hour pass very pleasantly, and they both commented on it with interest.

"I had an experience once myself something like that," said Stuart, with a pleased smile of recollection; "it happened in Paris"—he began with the deliberation of a man who is sure of his story—"and it turned out in much the same way. It didn't begin in Paris; it really began while we were crossing the English Channel to—"

"Oh, you mean about the Russian who took you for some one else and had you followed," said the Picture. "Yes, that was like it, except that in your case nothing happened."

Stuart took his cigar from between his lips and frowned severely at the lighted end for some little time before he spoke.

"My dear," he remonstrated, gently, "you mustn't tell me I've told you all my old stories before. It isn't fair. Now that I'm married, you see, I can't go about and have new experiences, and I've got to make use of the old ones."

"Oh, I'm so sorry," exclaimed the Picture, remorsefully. "I didn't mean to be rude. Please tell me about it. I should like to hear it again, ever so much. I *should* like to hear it again, really."

"Nonsense," said Stuart, laughing and shaking his head. "I was only joking; personally I hate people who tell long stories. That doesn't matter. I was thinking of something else."

He continued thinking of something else, which was, that though he had been in jest when he spoke of having given up the chance of meeting fresh experiences, he had nevertheless described a condition, and a painfully true one. His real life seemed to have stopped, and he saw himself in the future looking back and referring to it, as though it were the career of an entirely different person, of a young man, with quick sympathies which required satisfying, as any appetite requires food. And he had an uncomfortable doubt that these many ever-ready sympathies would rebel if fed on only one diet.

The Picture did not interrupt him in his thoughts, and he let his mind follow his eyes as they wandered over the objects above him on the mantle-shelf. They all meant something from the past—a busy, wholesome past which had formed habits of thought and action, habits he could no longer enjoy alone, and which, on the other hand, it was quite impossible for him to share with any one else. He was no longer to be alone.

Stuart stirred uneasily in his chair and poked at the fire before him.

"Do you remember the day you came to see me," said the Picture, sentimentally, "and built the fire yourself and lighted some girl's letters to make it burn?"

"Yes," said Stuart, "that is, I *said* that they were some girl's letters. It made it more picturesque. I am afraid they were bills. I should say I did remember it," he continued, enthusiastically. "You wore a black dress and little red slippers with big black rosettes, and you looked as beautiful as—as night—as a moonlight night."

The Picture frowned slightly.

"You are always telling me about how I looked," she complained; "can't you remember any time when we were together without remembering what I had on and how I appeared?"

"I cannot," said Stuart, promptly. "I can recall lots of other things besides, but I can't forget how you looked. You have a fashion of emphasizing episodes in that way which is entirely your own. But, as I say, I can remember something else. Do you remember, for instance, when we went up to West Point on that yacht? Wasn't it a grand day, with the autumn leaves on both sides of the Hudson, and the dress parade, and the dance afterward at the hotel?"

"Yes, I should think I did," said the Picture, smiling. "You spent all your time examining cannon, and talking to the men about 'firing in open order,' and left me all alone."

"Left you all alone! I like that," laughed Stuart; "all alone with about eighteen officers."

"Well, but that was natural," returned the Picture. "They were men. It's natural for a girl to talk to men, but why should a man want to talk to men?"

"Well, I know better than that now," said Stuart.

He proceeded to show that he knew better by remaining silent for the next half hour, during which time he continued to wonder whether this effort to keep up a conversation was not radically wrong. He thought of several things he might say, but he argued that it was an impossible situation where a man had to make conversation with his own wife.

The clock struck ten as he sat waiting, and he moved uneasily in his chair.

"What is it?" asked the Picture; "what makes you so restless?"

Stuart regarded the Picture timidly for a moment before he spoke. "I was just thinking," he said, doubtfully, "that we might run down after all, and take a look in at the last act; it's not too late even now. They're sure to run behind on the first night. And then," he urged, "we can go around and see Seldon. You have never been behind the scenes, have you? It's very interesting."

"No, I have not, but if we do," remonstrated the Picture, pathetically, "you *know* all those men will come trooping home with us. You know they will."

"But that's very complimentary," said Stuart. "Why, I like my friends to like my wife."

"Yes, but you know how they stay when they get here," she answered; "I don't believe they ever sleep. Don't you remember the last supper you gave me before we were married, when Mrs. Starr and you all were discussing Mr. Seldon's play? She didn't make a move to go until half past two, and I was *that* sleepy, I couldn't keep my eyes open."

"Yes," said Stuart, "I remember. I'm sorry. I thought it was very interesting. Seldon changed the whole second act on account of what she said. Well, after this," he laughed with cheerful desperation, "I think I shall make up for the part of a married man in a pair of slippers and a dressing-gown, and then perhaps I won't be tempted to roam abroad at night."

"You must wear the gown they are going to give you at Oxford," said the Picture, smiling placidly. "The one Aunt Lucy was telling me about. Why do they give you a gown?" she asked. "It seems such an odd thing to do."

"The gown comes with the degree, I believe," said Stuart.

"But why do they give *you* a degree?" persisted the Picture; "you never studied at Oxford, did you?"

Stuart moved slightly in his chair and shook his head. "I thought I told you," he said, gently. "No, I never studied there. I wrote some books on—things, and they liked them."

"Oh, yes, I remember now, you did tell me," said the Picture; "and I told Aunt Lucy about it, and said we would be in England during the season, when you got your degree, and she said you must be awfully clever to get it. You see—she does appreciate you, and you always treat her so distantly."

"Do I?" said Stuart; quietly; "I'm sorry."

"Will you have your portrait painted in it?" asked the Picture.

"In what?"

"In the gown. You are not listening," said the Picture,

reproachfully. "You ought to. Aunt Lucy says it's a beautiful shade of red silk, and very long. Is it?"

"I don't know," said Stuart, he shook his head, and dropping his chin into his hands, stared coldly down into the fire. He tried to persuade himself that he had been vainglorious, and that he had given too much weight to the honor which the University of Oxford would bestow upon him; that he had taken the degree too seriously, and that the Picture's view of it was the view of the rest of the world. But he could not convince himself that he was entirely at fault.

"Is it too late to begin on Guizot?" suggested his Picture, as an alternative to his plan. "It sounds so improving."

"Yes, it is much too late," answered Stuart, decidedly. "Besides, I don't want to be improved. I want to be amused, or inspired, or scolded. The chief good of friends is that they do one of these three things, and a wife should do all three."

"Which shall I do?" asked the Picture, smiling good-humoredly.

Stuart looked at the beautiful face and at the reclining figure of the woman to whom he was to turn for sympathy for the rest of his life, and felt a cold shiver of terror, that passed as quickly as it came. He reached out his hand and placed it on the arm of the chair where his wife's hand should have been, and patted the place kindly. He would shut his eyes to everything but that she was good and sweet and his wife. Whatever else she lacked that her beauty had covered up and hidden, and the want of which had lain unsuspected in their previous formal intercourse, could not be mended now. He would settle his step to hers, and eliminate all those interests from his life which were not hers as well. He had chosen a beautiful idol, and not a companion, for a wife. He had tried to warm his hands at the fire of a diamond.

Stuart's eyes closed wearily as though to shut out the memories of the past, or the foreknowledge of what the future was sure to be. His head sank forward on his breast, and with his hand shading his eyes, he looked beyond, through the dying fire, into the succeeding years.

The gay little French clock on the table sounded the hour of midnight briskly, with a pert insistent clamor, and at the same instant a boisterous and unruly knocking answered it from outside the library door.

Stuart rose uncertainly from his chair and surveyed the tiny clock face with a startled expression of bewilderment and relief.

"Stuart!" his friends called impatiently from the hall. "Stuart, let us in!" and without waiting further for recognition a merry company of gentlemen pushed their way noisily into the room.

"Where the devil have you been?" demanded Weimer. "You don't deserve to be spoken to at all after quitting us like that. But Seldon is so good-natured," he went on, "that he sent us after you. It was a great success, and he made a rattling good speech, and you missed the whole thing; and you ought to be ashamed of yourself. We've asked half the people in front to supper—two stray Englishmen, all the Wilton girls and their governor, and the chap that wrote the play. And Seldon and his brother Sam are coming as soon as they get their makeup off. Don't stand there like that, but hurry. What have you been doing?"

Stuart gave a nervous, anxious laugh. "Oh, don't ask me," he cried. "It was awful. I've been trying an experiment, and I had to keep it up until midnight, and—I'm so glad you fellows have come," he continued, halting midway in his explanation. "I *was* blue."

"You've been asleep in front of the fire," said young Sloane, "and you've been dreaming."

"Perhaps," laughed Stuart, gayly, "perhaps. But I'm awake now in any event. Sloane, old man," he cried, dropping both hands on the youngster's shoulders. "How much money have you? Enough to take me to Gibraltar? They can cable me the rest."

"Hoorah!" shouted Sloane, waltzing from one end of the

room to the other. "And we're off to Ab-yss-in-ia in the morn-ing," he sang. "There's plenty in my money belt," he cried, slapping his sides, "you can hear the ten-pound notes crackle whenever I breathe, and it's all yours, my dear boy, and welcome. And I'll prove to you that the Winchester is the better gun."

"All right," returned Stuart, gayly, "and I'll try to prove that the Italians don't know how to govern a native state. But who is giving this supper, anyway?" he demanded. "That is the main thing—that's what I want to know."

"You've got to pack, haven't you?" suggested Rives.

"I'll pack when I get back," said Stuart, struggling into his greatcoat, and searching in his pockets for his gloves. "Besides, my things are always ready and there's plenty of time, the boat doesn't leave for six hours yet."

"We'll all come back and help," said Weimer.

"Then I'll never get away," laughed Stuart. He was radiant, happy, and excited, like a boy back from school for the holidays. But when they had reached the pavement, he halted and ran his hand down into his pocket, as though feeling for his latch-key, and stood looking doubtfully at his friends.

"What is it now?" asked Rives, impatiently. "Have you forgotten something?"

Stuart looked back at the front door in momentary indecision.

"Y-es," he answered. "I did forget something. But it doesn't matter," he added, cheerfully, taking Sloane's arm.

"Come on," he said, "and so Seldon made a hit, did he? I am glad—and tell me, old man, how long will we have to wait at Gib for the P. & O.?"

Stuart's servant had heard the men trooping down the stairs, laughing and calling to one another as they went, and judging from this that they had departed for the night, he put out all the lights in the library and closed the piano, and lifted the windows to clear the room of the tobacco-smoke. He did not notice the beautiful photograph sitting upright in the armchair before the fireplace, and so left it alone in the deserted library.

The cold night-air swept in through the open window and chilled the silent room, and the dead coals in the grate dropped one by one into the fender with a dismal echoing clatter; but the Picture still sat in the armchair with the same graceful pose and the same lovely expression, and smiled sweetly at the encircling darkness.

THE EDITOR'S STORY

It was a warm afternoon in the early spring, and the air in the office was close and heavy. The letters of the morning had been answered and the proofs corrected, and the gentlemen who had come with ideas worth one column at space rates, and which they thought worth three, had compromised with the editor on a basis of two, and departed. The editor's desk was covered with manuscripts in a heap, a heap that never seemed to grow less, and each manuscript bore a character of its own, as marked or as unobtrusive as the character of the man or of the woman who had written it, which disclosed itself in the care with which some were presented for consideration, in the vain little ribbons of others, or the selfish manner in which still others were tightly rolled or vilely scribbled.

The editor held the first page of a poem in his hand, and was reading it mechanically, for its length had already declared against it, unless it might chance to be the precious gem out of a thousand, which must be chosen in spite of its twenty stanzas. But as the editor read, his interest awakened, and he scanned the verses again, as one would turn to look a second time at a face which seemed familiar. At the fourth stanza his memory was still in doubt, at the sixth it was warming to the chase, and at the end of the page was in full cry. He caught up the second page and looked for the final verse, and then at the name below, and then back again quickly to the title of the poem, and pushed aside the papers on his desk in search of any note which might have accompanied it.

The name signed at the bottom of the second page was Edwin Aram, the title of the poem was "Bohemia," and there was no accompanying note, only the name Berkeley written at the top of the first page. The envelope in which it had come gave no further clew. It was addressed in the same handwriting as that in which the poem had been written, and it bore the postmark of New York city. There was no request for the return of the poem, no direction to which either the poem itself or the check for its payment in the event of its acceptance might be sent. Berkeley might be the name of an apartment-house or of a country place or of a suburban town.

The editor stepped out of his office into the larger room beyond and said: "I've a poem here that appeared in an American magazine about seven years ago. I remember the date because I read it when I was at college. Some one is either trying to play a trick on us, or to get money by stealing some other man's brains."

It was in this way that Edwin Aram first introduced himself to our office, and while his poem was not accepted, it was not returned. On the contrary, Mr. Aram became to us one of the most interesting of our would-be contributors, and there was no author, no matter of what popularity, for whose work we waited with greater impatience. But Mr. Aram's personality still remained as completely hidden from us as were the productions which he offered from the sight of our subscribers. For each of the poems he sent had been stolen outright and signed with his name.

It was through no fault of ours that he continued to blush unseen, or that his pretty taste in poems was unappreciated by the general reader. We followed up every clew and every hint he chose to give us with an enthusiasm worthy of a search after a lost explorer, and with an animus worthy of better game. Yet there was some reason for our interest. The man who steals the work of another and who passes it off as his own is the special foe of every editor, but this particular editor had a personal distrust of Mr. Aram. He imagined that these poems might possibly be a trap which some one had laid for him with the purpose of drawing him into printing them, and then of pointing out by this fact how little read he was, and how unfit to occupy the swivel-chair into which he had so lately dropped. Or if this were not the case, the man was in any event the enemy of all honest people, who look unkindly on those who try to obtain money by false pretences.

The evasions of Edwin Aram were many, and his methods to

avoid detection not without skill. His second poem was written on a sheet of notepaper bearing the legend "The Shakespeare Debating Club. Edwin Aram, President."

This was intended to reassure us as to his literary taste and standard, and to meet any suspicion we might feel had there been no address of any sort accompanying the poem. No one we knew had ever heard of a Shakespeare Debating Club in New York city. But we gave him the benefit of the doubt until we found that this poem, like the first, was also stolen. His third poem bore his name and an address, which on instant inquiry turned out to be that of a vacant lot on Seventh Avenue near Central Park.

Edwin Aram had by this time become an exasperating and picturesque individual, and the editorial staff was divided in its opinion concerning him. It was argued on one hand that as the man had never sent us a real address, his object must be to gain a literary reputation at the expense of certain poets, and not to make money at ours. Others answered this by saying that fear of detection alone kept Edwin Aram from sending his real address, but that as soon as his poem was printed, and he ascertained by that fact that he had not been discovered, he would put in an application for payment, and let us know quickly enough to what portion of New York city his check should be forwarded.

This, however, presupposed the fact that he was writing to us over his real name, which we did not believe he would dare to do. No one in our little circle of journalists and literary men had ever heard of such a man, and his name did not appear in the directory. This fact, however, was not convincing in itself, as the residents of New York move from flat to hotel, and from apartments to boarding-houses as frequently as the Arab changes his camping-ground. We tried to draw him out at last by publishing a personal paragraph which stated that several contributions received from Edwin Aram would be returned to him if he would send stamps and his present address. The editor did not add that he would return the poems in person, but such was his warlike intention.

This had the desired result, and brought us a fourth poem and a fourth address, the name of a tall building which towers above Union Square. We seemed to be getting very warm now, and the editor gathered up the four poems, and called to his aid his friend Bronson, the ablest reporter on the New York ——, who was to act as chronicler. They took with them letters from the authors of two of the poems and from the editor of the magazine in which the first one had originally appeared, testifying to the fact that Edwin Aram had made an exact copy of the original, and wishing the brother editor good luck in catching the plagiarist.

The reporter looked these over with a critical eye. "The City Editor told me if we caught him," he said, "that I could let it run for all it was worth. I can use these names, I suppose, and I guess they have pictures of the poets at the office. If he turns out to be anybody in particular, it ought to be worth a full three columns. Sunday paper, too."

The amateur detectives stood in the lower hall in the tall building, between swinging doors, and jostled by hurrying hundreds, while they read the names on a marble directory.

"There he is!" said the editor, excitedly. "'American Literary Bureau.' One room on the fourteenth floor. That's just the sort of a place in which we would be likely to find him." But the reporter was gazing open-eyed at a name in large letters on an office door. "Edward K. Aram," it read, "Commissioner of ——, and City ——."

"What do you think of *that?*" he gasped, triumphantly.

"Nonsense," said the editor. "He wouldn't dare; besides, the initials are different. You're expecting too good a story."

"That's the way to get them," answered the reporter, as he hurried towards the office of the City ——. "If a man falls dead, believe it's a suicide until you prove it's not; if you find a suicide, believe it's a murder until you are convinced to the contrary. Otherwise you'll get beaten. We don't want the proprietor of a little literary bureau, we want a big city official and I'll believe we have one until he proves we haven't."

"Which are you going to ask for?" whispered the editor, "Edward K. or Edwin?"

"Edwin, I should say," answered the reporter. "He has probably given notice that mail addressed that way should go to him."

"Is Mr. Edwin Aram in?" he asked.

A clerk raised his head and looked behind him. "No," he said; "his desk is closed. I guess he's gone home for the day."

The reporter nudged the editor savagely with his elbow, but his face gave no sign. "That's a pity," he said; "we have an appointment with him. He still lives at Sixty-first Street and Madison Avenue, I believe, does he not?"

"No," said the clerk; "that's his father, the Commissioner, Edward K. The son lives at ——. Take the Sixth Avenue elevated and get off at 116th Street."

"Thank you," said the reporter. He turned a triumphant smile upon the editor. "We've got him!" he said, excitedly. "And the son of old Edward K., too! Think of it! Trying to steal a few dollars by cribbing other men's poems; that's the best story there has been in the papers for the past three months—'Edward K. Aram's son a thief!' Look at the names—politicians, poets, editors, all mixed up in it. It's good for three columns, sure."

"We've got to think of his people, too," urged the editor, as they mounted the steps of the elevated road.

"He didn't think of them," said the reporter.

The house in which Mr. Aram lived was an apartment-house, and the brass latchets in the hallway showed that it contained three suites. There were visiting-cards under the latchets of the first and third stories, and under that of the second a piece of notepaper on which was written the autograph of Edwin Aram. The editor looked at it curiously. He had never believed it to be a real name.

"I am sorry Edwin Aram did not turn out to be a woman," he

said, regretfully; "it would have been so much more interesting."

"Now," instructed Bronson, impressively, "whether he is in or not we have him. If he's not in, we wait until he comes, even if he doesn't come until morning; we don't leave this place until we have seen him."

"Very well," said the editor.

The maid left them standing at the top of the stairs while she went to ask if Mr. Aram was in, and whether he would see two gentlemen who did not give their names because they were strangers to him. The two stood silent while they waited, eying each other anxiously, and when the girl reopened the door, nodded pleasantly, and said, "Yes, Mr. Aram is in," they hurried past her as though they feared that he would disappear in midair, or float away through the windows before they could reach him.

And yet, when they stood at last face-to-face him, he bore a most disappointing air of everyday respectability. He was a tall, thin young man, with light hair and mustache and large blue eyes. His back was towards the window, so that his face was in the shadow, and he did not rise as they entered. The room in which he sat was a prettily furnished one, opening into another tiny room, which, from the number of books in it, might have been called a library. The rooms had a well-to-do, even prosperous, air, but they did not show any evidences of a pronounced taste on the part of their owner, either in the way in which they were furnished or in the decorations of the walls. A little girl of about seven or eight years of age, who was standing between her father's knees, with a hand on each, and with her head thrown back on his shoulder, looked up at the two visitors with evident interest, and smiled brightly.

"Mr. Aram?" asked the editor, tentatively.

The young man nodded, and the two visitors seated themselves.

"I wish to talk to you on a matter of private business," the editor began. "Wouldn't it be better to send the little girl away?"

The child shook her head violently at this, and crowded up closely to her father; but he held her away from him gently, and told her to "run and play with Annie."

She passed the two visitors, with her head held scornfully in air, and left the men together. Mr. Aram seemed to have a most passive and incurious disposition. He could have no idea as to who his anonymous visitors might be, nor did he show any desire to know.

"I am the editor of —," the editor began. "My friend also writes for that periodical. I have received several poems from you lately, Mr. Aram, and one in particular which we all liked very much. It was called 'Bohemia.' But it is so like one that has appeared under the same title in the '— Magazine' that I thought I would see you about it, and ask you if you could explain the similarity. You see," he went on, "it would be less embarrassing if you would do so now than later, when the poem has been published and when people might possibly accuse you of plagiarism." The editor smiled encouragingly and waited.

Mr. Aram crossed one leg over the other and folded his hands in his lap. He exhibited no interest, and looked drowsily at the editor. When he spoke it was in a tone of unstudied indifference. "I never wrote a poem called 'Bohemia,'" he said, slowly; "at least, if I did I don't remember it."

The editor had not expected a flat denial, and it irritated him, for he recognized it to be the safest course the man could pursue, if he kept to it. "But you don't mean to say," he protested, smiling, "that you can write so excellent a poem as 'Bohemia' and then forget having done so?"

"I might," said Mr. Aram, unresentfully, and with little interest. "I scribble a good deal."

"Perhaps," suggested the reporter, politely, with the air of one who is trying to cover up a difficulty to the satisfaction of all, "Mr. Aram would remember it if he saw it."

The editor nodded his head in assent, and took the first page of the two on which the poem was written, and held it out to Mr. Aram, who accepted the piece of foolscap and eyed it listlessly.

"Yes, I wrote that," he said. "I copied it out of a book called *Gems from American Poets*." There was a lazy pause. "But I never sent it to any paper." The editor and the reporter eyed each other with outward calm but with some inward astonishment. They could not see why he had not adhered to his original denial of the thing *in toto*. It seemed to them so foolish, to admit having copied the poem and then to deny having forwarded it.

"You see," explained Mr. Aram, still with no apparent interest in the matter, "I am very fond of poetry; I like to recite it, and I often write it out in order to make me remember it. I find it impresses the words on my mind. Well, that's what has happened. I have copied this poem out at the office probably, and one of the clerks there has found it, and has supposed that I wrote it, and he has sent it to your paper as a sort of a joke on me. You see, father being so well-known, it would rather amuse the boys if I came out as a poet. That's how it was, I guess. Somebody must have found it and sent it to you, because *I* never sent it."

There was a moment of thoughtful consideration. "I see," said the editor. "I used to do that same thing myself when I had to recite pieces at school. I found that writing the verses down helped me to remember them. I remember that I once copied out many of Shakespeare's sonnets. But, Mr. Aram, it never occurred to me, after having copied out one of Shakespeare's sonnets, to sign my own name at the bottom of it."

Mr. Aram's eyes dropped to the page of manuscript in his hand and rested there for some little time. Then he said, without raising his head, "I haven't signed this."

"No," replied the editor; "but you signed the second page, which I still have in my hand."

The editor and his companion expected some expression of

indignation from Mr. Aram at this, some question of their right to come into his house and cross-examine him and to accuse him, tentatively at least, of literary fraud, but they were disappointed. Mr. Aram's manner was still one of absolute impassibility. Whether this manner was habitual to him they could not know, but it made them doubt their own judgment in having so quickly accused him, as it bore the look of undismayed innocence.

It was the reporter who was the first to break the silence. "Perhaps some one has signed Mr. Aram's name—the clerk who sent it, for instance."

Young Mr. Aram looked up at him curiously, and held out his hand for the second page. "Yes," he drawled, "that's how it happened. That's not my signature. I never signed that."

The editor was growing restless. "I have several other poems here from you," he said; "one written from the rooms of the Shakespeare Debating Club, of which I see you are president. Your clerk could not have access there, could he? He did not write that, too?"

"No," said Mr. Aram, doubtfully, "he could not have written that."

The editor handed him the poem. "It's yours, then?"

"Yes, that's mine," Mr. Aram replied.

"And the signature?"

"Yes, and the signature. I wrote that myself," Mr. Aram explained, "and sent it myself. That other one ('Bohemia') I just copied out to remember, but this is original with me."

"And the envelope in which it was enclosed," asked the editor, "did you address that also?"

Mr. Aram examined it uninterestedly. "Yes, that's my handwriting too." He raised his head. His face wore an expression of patient politeness.

"Oh!" exclaimed the editor, suddenly, in some embarrassment. "I handed you the wrong envelope. I beg your pardon. That envelope is the one in which 'Bohemia' came."

The reporter gave a hardly perceptible start; his eyes were fixed on the pattern of the rug at his feet, and the editor continued to examine the papers in his hand. There was a moment's silence. From outside came the noise of children playing in the street and the rapid rush of a passing wagon.

When the two visitors raised their heads Mr. Aram was looking at them strangely, and the fingers folded in his lap were twisting in and out.

"This Shakespeare Debating Club," said the editor, "where are its rooms, Mr. Aram?"

"It has no rooms, now," answered the poet. "It has disbanded. It never had any regular rooms; we just met about and read."

"I see—exactly," said the editor. "And the house on Seventh Avenue from which your third poem was sent—did you reside there then, or have you always lived here?"

"No, yes—I used to live there—I lived there when I wrote that poem."

The editor looked at the reporter and back at Mr. Aram. "It is a vacant lot, Mr. Aram," he said, gravely.

There was a long pause. The poet rocked slowly up and down in his rocking-chair, and looked at his hands, which he rubbed over one another as though they were cold. Then he raised his head and cleared his throat.

"Well, gentlemen," he said, "you have made out your case."

"Yes," said the editor, regretfully, "we have made out our case." He could not help but wish that the fellow had stuck to his original denial. It was too easy a victory.

"I don't say, mind you," went on Mr. Aram, "that I ever took anybody's verses and sent them to a paper as my own, but I ask you, as one gentleman talking to another, and inquiring for information, what is there wrong in doing it? I say, *if* I had done it, which I don't admit I ever did, where's the harm?"

"Where's the harm?" cried the two visitors in chorus.

"Obtaining money under false pretences," said the editor, "is the harm you do the publishers, and robbing another man of the work of his brain and what credit belongs to him is the harm you do him, and telling a lie is the least harm done. Such a contemptible foolish lie, too, that you might have known would surely find you out in spite of the trouble you took to—"

"I never asked you for any money," interrupted Mr. Aram, quietly.

"But we would have sent it to you, nevertheless," retorted the editor, "if we had not discovered in time that the poems were stolen."

"Where would you have sent it?" asked Mr. Aram. "I never gave you a right address, did I? I ask you, did I?"

The editor paused in some confusion, "Well, if you did not want the money, what did you want?" he exclaimed. "I must say I should like to know."

Mr. Aram rocked himself to and fro, and gazed at his two inquisitors with troubled eyes. "I didn't see any harm in it then," he repeated. "I don't see any harm in it now. I didn't ask you for any money. I sort of thought," he said, confusedly, "that I should like to see my name in print. I wanted my friends to see it. I'd have liked to have shown it to—to—well, I'd like my wife to have seen it. She's interested in literature and books and magazines and things like that. That was all I wanted. That's why I did it."

The reporter looked up askance at the editor, as a prompter watches the actor to see if he is ready to take his cue.

"How do I know that?" demanded the editor, sharply. He found it somewhat difficult to be severe with this poet, for the man admitted so much so readily, and would not defend himself. Had he only blustered and grown angry and ordered them out, instead of sitting helplessly there rocking to and fro and picking at the back of his hands, it would have made it so much easier. "How do we know," repeated the editor, "that you did not intend to wait until the poems had appeared, and then send us your real address and ask for the money, saying that you had moved since you had last written us?"

"Oh," protested Mr. Aram, "you know I never thought of that."

"I don't know anything of the sort," said the editor. "I only know that you have forged and lied and tried to obtain money that doesn't belong to you, and that I mean to make an example of you and frighten other men from doing the same thing. No editor has read every poem that was ever written, and there is no protection for him from such fellows as you, and the only thing he can do when he does catch one of you is to make an example of him. That's what I am going to do. I am going to make an example of you. I am going to nail you up as people nail up dead crows to frighten off the live ones. It is my intention to give this to the papers tonight, and you know what they will do with it in the morning."

There was a long and most uncomfortable pause, and it is doubtful if the editor did not feel it as much as did the man opposite him. The editor turned to his friend for a glance of sympathy, or of disapproval even, but that gentleman still sat bending forward with his eyes fixed on the floor, while he tapped with the top of his cane against his teeth.

"You don't mean," said Mr. Aram, in a strangely different voice from which he had last spoken, "that you would do that?"

"Yes, I do," blustered the editor. But even as he spoke he was conscious of a sincere regret that he had not come alone. He could intuitively feel Bronson mapping out the story in his mind and memorizing Aram's every word, and taking mental notes of the framed certificates of high membership in different military and masonic associations which hung upon the walls. It had not been long since the editor was himself a reporter, and he could see that it was as good a story as Bronson could wish it to be. But he reiterated, "Yes, I mean to give it to the papers tonight."

"But think," said Aram—"think, sir, who I am. You don't want to ruin me for the rest of my life just for a matter of fifteen dollars, do you? Fifteen dollars that no one has lost, either. If I'd embezzled a million or so, or if I had robbed the city, well and good! I'd have taken big risks for big money; but you are going to punish me just as hard, because I tried to please my wife, as though I had robbed a mint. No one has really been hurt," he pleaded; "the men who wrote the poems—they've been paid for them; they've got all the credit for them they *can* get. You've not lost a cent. I've gained nothing by it; and yet you gentlemen are going to give this thing to the papers, and, as you say, sir, we know what they will make of it. What with my being my father's son, and all that, my father is going to suffer. My family is going to suffer. It will ruin me—"

The editor put the papers back into his pocket. If Bronson had not been there he might possibly instead have handed them over to Mr. Aram, and this story would never have been written. But he could not do that now. Mr. Aram's affairs had become the property of the New York newspaper.

He turned to his friend doubtfully. "What do you think, Bronson?" he asked.

At this sign of possible leniency Aram ceased in his rocking and sat erect, with eyes wide open and fixed on Bronson's face. But the latter trailed his stick over the rug beneath his feet and shrugged his shoulders.

"Mr. Aram," he said, "might have thought of his family and his father before he went into this business. It is rather late now. But," he added, "I don't think it is a matter we can decide in any event. It should be left to the firm."

"Yes," said the editor, hurriedly, glad of the excuse to temporize, "we must leave it to the house." But he read Bronson's answer to mean that he did not intend to let the plagiarist escape, and he knew that even were Bronson willing to do so, there was still his City Editor to be persuaded.

The two men rose and stood uncomfortably, shifting their hats in their hands—and avoiding each other's eyes. Mr. Aram stood up also, and seeing that his last chance had come, began again to plead desperately.

"What good would fifteen dollars do me?" he said, with a gesture of his hands round the room. "I don't have to look for money as hard as that I tell you," he reiterated, "it wasn't the money I wanted. I didn't mean any harm. I didn't know it was wrong. I just wanted to please my wife—that was all. My God, man, can't you see that you are punishing me out of all proportion?"

The visitors walked towards the door, and he followed them, talking the faster as they drew near to it. The scene had become an exceedingly painful one, and they were anxious to bring it to a close.

The editor interrupted him. "We will let you know," he said, "what we have decided to do by tomorrow morning."

"You mean," retorted the man, hopelessly and reproachfully, "that I will read it in the Sunday papers."

Before the editor could answer they heard the door leading into the apartment open and close, and some one stepping quickly across the hall to the room in which they stood. The entrance to the room was hung with a portière, and as the three men paused in silence this portière was pushed back, and a young lady stood in the doorway, holding the curtains apart with her two hands. She was smiling, and the smile lighted a face that was inexpressibly bright and honest and true. Aram's face had been lowered, but the eyes of the other two men were staring wide open towards the unexpected figure, which seemed to bring a taste of fresh pure air into the feverish atmosphere of the place. The girl stopped uncertainly when she saw the two strangers, and bowed her head slightly as the mistress of a house might welcome any one whom she found in her drawing-room. She was entirely above and apart from her surroundings. It was not only that she was exceedingly pretty, but that everything about her, from her attitude to her cloth walking-dress, was significant of good taste and high breeding.

She paused uncertainly, still smiling, and with her gloved hands holding back the curtains and looking at Aram with eyes filled with a kind confidence. She was apparently waiting for him to present his friends.

The editor made a sudden but irrevocable resolve. "If she is only a chance visitor," he said to himself, "I will still expose him; but if that woman in the doorway is his wife, I will push Bronson under the elevated train, and the secret will die with me."

What Bronson's thoughts were he could not know, but he was conscious that his friend had straightened his broad shoulders and was holding his head erect.

Aram raised his face, but he did not look at the woman in the door. "In a minute, dear," he said; "I am busy with these gentlemen."

The girl gave a little "oh" of apology, smiled at her husband's bent head, inclined her own again slightly to the other men, and let the portière close behind her. It had been as dramatic an entrance and exit as the two visitors had ever seen upon the stage. It was as if Aram had given a signal, and the only person who could help him had come in the nick of time to plead for him. Aram, stupid as he appeared to be, had evidently felt the effect his wife's appearance had made upon his judges. He still kept his eyes fixed upon the floor, but he said, and this time with more confidence in his tone:—

"It is not, gentlemen, as though I were an old man. I have so very long to live—so long to try to live this down. Why, I am as young as you are. How would you like to have a thing like this to carry with you till you died?"

The editor still stood staring blankly at the curtains through which Mr. Aram's good angel, for whom he had lied and cheated in order to gain credit in her eyes, had disappeared. He pushed them aside with his stick. "We will let you know tomorrow morning," he repeated, and the two men passed out from the poet's presence, and on into the hall. They descended the stairs in an uncomfortable silence, Bronson leading the way, and the editor endeavoring to read his verdict by the back of his head and shoulders.

At the foot of the steps he pulled his friend by the sleeve. "Bronson," he coaxed, "you are not going to use it, are you?"

Bronson turned on him savagely. "For Heaven's sake!" he protested, "what do you think I am; did you *see* her?"

So the New York — lost a very good story, and Bronson a large sum of money for not writing it, and Mr. Aram was taught a lesson, and his young wife's confidence in him remained unshaken. The editor and reporter dined together that night, and over their cigars decided with sudden terror that Mr. Aram might, in his ignorance of their good intentions concerning him, blow out his brains, and for nothing. So they despatched a messenger-boy up town in post-haste with a note saying that "the firm" had decided to let the matter drop. Although, perhaps, it would have been better to have given him one sleepless night at least.

That was three years ago, and since then Mr. Aram's father has fallen out with Tammany, and has been retired from public service. Bronson has been sent abroad to represent the United States at a foreign court, and has asked the editor to write the story that he did not write, but with such changes in the names of people and places that no one save Mr. Aram may know who Mr. Aram really was and is.

This the editor has done, reporting what happened as faithfully as he could, and in the hope that it will make an interesting story in spite of the fact, and not on account of the fact, that it is a true one.

AN ASSISTED EMIGRANT

Guido stood on the curbstone in Fourteenth Street, between Fifth Avenue and Sixth Avenue, with a row of plaster figures drawn up on the sidewalk in front of him. It was snowing, and they looked cold in consequence, especially the Night and Morning. A line of men and boys stretched on either side of Guido all along the curbstone, with toys and dolls, and guns that shot corks into the air with a loud report, and glittering dressings for the Christmas trees. It was the day before Christmas. The man who stood next in line to Guido had hideous black monkeys that danced from the end of a rubber string. The man danced up and down too, very much, so Guido thought, as the monkeys did, and stamped his feet on the icy pavement, and shouted: "Here yer are, lady, for five cents. Take them home to the children." There were hundreds and hundreds of ladies and little girls crowding by all of the time; some of them were a little cross and a little tired, as if Christmas shopping had told on their nerves, but the greater number were happy-looking and warm, and some stopped and laughed at the monkeys dancing on the rubber strings, and at the man with the frost on his mustache, who jumped too, and cried, "Only five cents, lady—nice Christmas presents for the children."

Sometimes the ladies bought the monkeys, but no one looked at the cold plaster figures of St. Joseph, and Diana, and Night and Morning, nor at the heads of Mars and Minerva—not even at the figure of the Virgin, with her two hands held out, which Guido pressed in his arms against his breast.

Guido had been in New York city just one month. He was very young—so young that he had never done anything at home but sit on the wharves and watch the ships come in and out of the great harbor of Genoa. He never had wished to depart with these ships when they sailed away, nor wondered greatly as to where they went. He was content with the wharves and with the narrow streets near by, and to look up from the bulkheads at the sailors working in the rigging, and the 'long-shoremen rolling the casks on board, or lowering great square boxes into the holds.

He would have liked, could he have had his way, to live so for the rest of his life; but they would not let him have his way, and coaxed him on a ship to go to the New World to meet his uncle. He was not a real uncle, but only a make-believe one, to satisfy those who objected to assisted immigrants, and who wished to be assured against having to support Guido, and others like him. But they were not half so anxious to keep Guido at home as he himself was to stay there.

The new uncle met him at Ellis Island, and embraced him affectionately, and put him in an express wagon, and drove him with a great many more of his countrymen to where Mulberry Street makes a bend and joins Hester. And in the Bend Guido found thousands of his fellows sleeping twenty in a room and over-crowded into the street: some who had but just arrived, and others who had already learned to swear in English, and had their street-cleaning badges and their peddler's licenses, to show that they had not been overlooked by the kindly society of Tammany, which sees that no free and independent voter shall go unrewarded.

New York affected Guido like a bad dream. It was cold and muddy, and the snow when it fell turned to mud so quickly that Guido believed they were one and the same. He did not dare to think of the place he know as home. And the sight of the colored advertisements of the steamship lines that hung in the windows of the Italian bankers hurt him as the sound of traffic on the street cuts to the heart of a prisoner in the Tombs. Many of his countrymen bade good-by to Mulberry Street and sailed away; but they had grown rich through obeying the padrones, and working night and morning sweeping the Avenue uptown, and by living on the refuse from the scows at Canal Street. Guido never hoped to grow rich, and no one stopped to buy his uncle's wares.

The electric lights came out, and still the crowd passed and thronged before him, and the snow fell and left no mark on the white figures. Guido was growing cold, and the bustle of the hurrying hundreds which had entertained him earlier in the day had ceased to interest him, and his amusement had given place to the fear that no one of them would ever stop, and that he would return to his uncle empty-handed. He was hungry now, as well as cold, and though there was not much rich food in the Bend at any time, today he had had nothing of any quality to eat since early morning. The man with the monkeys turned his head from time to time, and spoke to him in a language that he could not understand; although he saw that it was something amusing and well meant that the man said, and so smiled back and nodded. He felt it to be quite a loss when the man moved away.

Guido thought very slowly, but he at last began to feel a certain contempt for the stiff statues and busts which no one wanted, and buttoned the figure of the one of the woman with her arms held out, inside of his jacket, and tucked his scarf in around it, so that it might not be broken, and also that it might not bear the ignominy with the others of being overlooked. Guido was a gentle, slow-thinking boy, and could not have told you why he did this, but he knew that this figure was of different clay from the others. He had seen it placed high in the cathedrals at home, and he had been told that if you ask certain things of it it will listen to you.

The women and children began to disappear from the crowd, and the necessity of selling some of his wares impressed itself more urgently upon him as the night grew darker and possible customers fewer. He decided that he had taken up a bad position, and that instead of waiting for customers to come to him, he ought to go seek for them. With this purpose in his mind, he gathered the figures together upon his tray, and resting it upon his shoulder, moved further along the street, to Broadway, where the crowd was greater and the shops more brilliantly lighted. He had good cause to be watchful, for the sidewalks were slippery with ice, and the people rushed and hurried and brushed past him without noticing the burden he carried on one shoulder. He wished now that he knew some words of this new language, that he might call his wares and challenge the notice of the passers-by, as did the other men who shouted so continually and vehemently at the hurrying crowds. He did not know what might happen if he failed to sell one of his statues; it was a possibility so awful that he did not dare conceive of its punishment. But he could do nothing, and so stood silent, dumbly presenting his tray to the people near him.

His wanderings brought him to the corner of a street, and he started to cross it, in the hope of better fortune in untried territory. There was no need of his hurrying to do this, although a car was coming towards him, so he stepped carefully but surely. But as he reached the middle of the track a man came towards him from the opposite pavement; they met and hesitated, and then both jumped to the same side, and the man's shoulder struck the tray and threw the white figures flying to the track, where the horses tramped over them on their way. Guido fell backwards, frightened and shaken, and the car stopped, and the driver and the conductor leaned out anxiously from each end.

There seemed to be hundreds of people all around Guido, and some of them picked him up and asked him questions in a very loud voice, as though that would make the language they spoke more intelligible. Two men took him by each arm and talked with him in earnest tones, and punctuated their questions by shaking him gently. He could not answer them, but only sobbed, and beat his hands softly together, and looked about him for a chance to escape. The conductor of the car jerked the strap violently, and the car went on its way. Guido watched the conductor, as he stood with his hands in his pockets looking back at him. Guido had a confused idea that the people on the car might pay him for the plaster figures which had been scattered in the slush and snow, so that the heads and arms and legs lay on every side or were ground into heaps of white powder. But when the car disappeared into the night he gave up this hope, and pulling himself free from his captor, slipped through the crowd and ran off into a side street. A man who had seen the accident had been trying to take up a collection in the crowd, which had grown less sympathetic and less numerous in consequence, and had gathered more than the plaster casts were worth; but Guido did not know this, and when they came to look for him he was gone, and the bareheaded gentleman, with his hat full of coppers and dimes, was left in much embarrassment.

Guido walked to Washington Square, and sat down on a bench to rest, and then curled over quickly, and stretching himself out at full length, wept bitterly. When any one passed he held his breath and pretended to be asleep. He did not know what he was to do or where he was to go. Such a calamity as this had never entered into his calculations of the evils which might overtake him, and it overwhelmed him utterly. A policeman touched him with his nightstick, and spoke to him kindly enough, but the boy only backed away from the man until he was out of his reach, and then ran on again, slipping and stumbling on the ice and snow. He ran to Christopher Street, through Greenwich Village, and on to the wharves.

It was quite late, and he had recovered from his hunger, and only felt a sick tired ache at his heart. His feet were heavy and numb, and he was very sleepy. People passed him continually, and doors opened into churches and into noisy glaring saloons and crowded shops, but it did not seem possible to him that there could be any relief from any source for the sorrow that had befallen him. It seemed too awful, and as impossible to mend as it would be to bring the crushed plaster into shape again. He considered dully that his uncle would miss him and wait for him, and that his anger would increase with every moment of his delay. He felt that he could never return to his uncle again.

Then he came to another park, opening into a square, with

lighted saloons on one side, and on the other great sheds, with ships lying beside them, and the electric lights showing their spars and masts against the sky. It had ceased snowing, but the air from the river was piercing and cold, and swept through the wires overhead with a ceaseless moaning. The numbness had crept from his feet up over the whole extent of his little body, and he dropped upon a flight of steps back of a sailors' boarding-house, and shoved his hands inside of his jacket for possible warmth. His fingers touched the figure he had hidden there and closed upon it lightly, and then his head dropped back against the wall, and he fell into a heavy sleep. The night passed on and grew colder, and the wind came across the ice-blocked river with shriller, sharper blasts, but Guido did not hear it.

"Chuckey" Martin, who blacked boots in front of the corner saloon in summer and swept out the bar-room in winter, came out through the family entrance and dumped a pan of hot ashes into the snowbank, and then turned into the house with a shiver. He saw a mass of something lying curled up on the steps of the next house, and remembered it after he had closed the door of the family entrance behind him and shoved the pan under the stove. He decided at last that it might be one of the saloon's customers, or a stray sailor with loose change in his pockets, which he would not miss when he awoke. So he went out again, and picking Guido up, brought him in in his arms and laid him out on the floor.

There were over thirty men in the place; they had been celebrating the coming of Christmas; and three of them pushed each other out of the way in their eagerness to pour very bad brandy between Guido's teeth. "Chuckey" Martin felt a sense of proprietorship in Guido, by the right of discovery, and resented this, pushing them away, and protesting that the thing to do was to rub his feet with snow.

A fat oily chief engineer of an Italian tramp steamer dropped on his knees beside Guido and beat the boy's hands, and with unsteady fingers tore open his scarf and jacket, and as he did this the figure of the plaster Virgin with her hands stretched out looked up at him from its bed on Guido's chest.

Some of the sailors drew their hands quickly across their breasts, and others swore in some alarm, and the barkeeper drank the glass of whiskey he had brought for Guido at a gulp, and then readjusted his apron to show that nothing had disturbed his equanimity. Guido sat up, with his head against the chief engineer's knees, and opened his eyes, and his ears were greeted with words in his own tongue. They gave him hot coffee and hot soup and more brandy, and he told his story in a burst of words that flowed like a torrent of tears—how he had been stolen from his home at Genoa, where he used to watch the boats from the stone pier in front of the custom-house, at which the sailors nodded, and how the padrone, who was not his uncle, finding he could not black boots nor sell papers, had given him these plaster casts to sell, and how he had whipped him when people would not buy them, and how at last he had tripped, and broken them all except this one hidden in his breast, and how he had gone to sleep, and he asked now why had they wakened him, for he had no place to go.

Guido remembered telling them this, and following them by their gestures as they retold it to the others in a strange language, and then the lights began to spin, and the faces grew distant, and he reached out his hand for the fat chief engineer, and felt his arms tightening around him.

A cold wind woke Guido, and the sound of something throbbing and beating like a great clock. He was very warm and tired and lazy, and when he raised his head he touched the ceiling close above him, and when he opened his eyes he found himself in a little room with a square table covered with oilcloth in the centre, and rows of beds like shelves around the walls. The room rose and fell as the streets did when he had had nothing to eat, and he scrambled out of the warm blankets and crawled fearfully up a flight of narrow stairs.

There was water on either side of him, beyond and behind him—water blue and white and dancing in the sun, with great blocks of dirty ice tossing on its surface.

And behind him lay the odious city of New York, with its great bridge and high buildings, and before him the open sea. The chief engineer crawled up from the engine-room and came towards him, rubbing the perspiration from his face with a dirty towel.

"Good-morning," he called out. "You are feeling pretty well?"

"Yes."

"It is Christmas day. Do you know where you are going? You are going to Italy, to Genoa. It is over there," he said, pointing with his finger. "Go back to your bed and keep warm."

He picked Guido up in his arms, and ran with him down the companionway, and tossed him back into his berth. Then he pointed to the shelf at one end of the little room, above the sheet-iron stove. The plaster figure that Guido had wrapped in his breast had been put there and lashed to its place.

"That will bring us good luck and a quick voyage," said the chief engineer.

Guido lay quite still until the fat engineer had climbed up the companionway again and permitted the sunlight to once more enter the cabin. Then he crawled out of his berth and dropped on his knees, and raised up his hands to the plaster figure which no one would buy.

THE REPORTER
WHO MADE HIMSELF KING

The Old Time Journalist will tell you that the best reporter is the one who works his way up. He holds that the only way to start is as a printer's devil or as an office boy, to learn in time to set type, to graduate from a compositor into a stenographer, and as a stenographer take down speeches at public meetings, and so finally grow into a real reporter, with a fire badge on your left suspender, and a speaking acquaintance with all the greatest men in the city, not even excepting Police Captains.

That is the old time journalist's idea of it. That is the way he was trained, and that is why at the age of sixty he is still a reporter. If you train up a youth in this way, he will go into reporting with too full a knowledge of the newspaper business, with no illusions concerning it, and with no ignorant enthusiasms, but with a keen and justifiable impression that he is not paid enough for what he does. And he will only do what he is paid to do.

Now, you cannot pay a good reporter for what he does, because he does not work for pay. He works for his paper. He gives his time, his health, his brains, his sleeping hours, and his eating hours, and sometimes his life to get news for it. He thinks the sun rises only that men may have light by which to read it. But if he has been in a newspaper office from his youth up, he finds out before he becomes a reporter that this is not so, and loses his real value. He should come right out of the University where he has been doing "campus notes" for the college weekly, and be pitchforked out into city work without knowing whether the Battery is at Harlem or Hunter's Point, and with the idea that he is a Moulder of Public Opinion and that the Power of the Press is greater than the Power of Money, and that the few lines he writes are of more value in the Editor's eyes than is the column of advertising on the last page, which they are not.

After three years—it is sometimes longer, sometimes not so long—he finds out that he has given his nerves and his youth and his enthusiasm in exchange for a general fund of miscellaneous knowledge, the opportunity of personal encounter with all the greatest and most remarkable men and events that have risen in those three years, and a great fund of resource and patience. He will find that he has crowded the experiences of the lifetime of the ordinary young business man, doctor, or lawyer, or man about town, into three short years; that he has learned to think and to act quickly, to be patient and unmoved when every one else has lost his head, actually or figuratively speaking; to write as fast as another man can talk, and to be able to talk with authority on matters of which other men do not venture even to think until they have read what he has written with a copy-boy at his elbow on the night previous.

It is necessary for you to know this, that you may understand what manner of man young Albert Gordon was.

Young Gordon had been a reporter just three years. He had left Yale when his last living relative died, and had taken the morning train for New York, where they had promised him reportorial work on one of the innumerable Greatest New York Dailies. He arrived at the office at noon, and was sent back over the same road on which he had just come, to Spuyten Duyvil, where a train had been wrecked and everybody of consequence to suburban New York killed. One of the old reporters hurried him to the office again with his "copy," and after he had delivered that, he was sent to the Tombs to talk French to a man in Murderer's Row, who could not talk anything else, but who had shown some international skill in the use of a jimmy. And at eight, he covered a flower-show in Madison Square Garden; and at eleven was sent over the Brooklyn Bridge in a cab to watch a fire and make guesses at the losses to the insurance companies.

He went to bed at one, and dreamed of shattered locomotives, human beings lying still with blankets over them, rows of cells, and banks of beautiful flowers nodding their heads to the tunes of the brass band in the gallery. He decided when he awoke the next morning that he had entered upon a picturesque and exciting career, and as one day followed another, he became more and more convinced of it, and more and more devoted to it. He was twenty then, and he was now twenty-three, and in that time had become a great reporter, and had been to Presidential conventions in Chicago, revolutions in Hayti, Indian outbreaks on the Plains, and midnight meetings of moonlighters in Tennessee, and had seen what work earthquakes, floods, fire, and fever could do in great cities, and had contradicted the President, and borrowed matches from burglars. And now he thought he would like to rest and breathe a bit, and not to work again unless as a war correspondent. The only obstacle to his becoming a great war correspondent lay in the fact that there was no war, and a war correspondent without a war is about as absurd an individual as a general without an army. He read the papers every morning on the elevated trains for war clouds; but though there were many war clouds, they always drifted apart, and peace smiled again. This was very disappointing to young Gordon, and he became more and more keenly discouraged.

And then as war work was out of the question, he decided to write his novel. It was to be a novel of New York life, and he wanted a quiet place in which to work on it. He was already making inquiries among the suburban residents of his acquaintance for just such a quiet spot, when he received an offer to go to the Island of Opeki in the North Pacific Ocean, as secretary to the American consul to that place. The gentleman who had been appointed by the President to act as consul at Opeki, was Captain Leonard T. Travis, a veteran of the Civil War, who had contracted a severe attack of rheumatism while camping out at night in the dew, and who on account of this souvenir of his efforts to save the Union had allowed the Union he had saved to support him in one office or another ever since. He had met young Gordon at a dinner, and had had the presumption to ask him to serve as his secretary, and Gordon, much to his surprise, had accepted his offer. The idea of a quiet life in the tropics with new and beautiful surroundings, and with nothing to do and plenty of time in which to do it, and to write his novel besides, seemed to Albert to be just what he wanted; and though he did not know nor care much for his superior officer, he agreed to go with him promptly, and proceeded to say good-by to his friends and to make his preparations. Captain Travis was so delighted with getting such a clever young gentleman for his secretary, that he referred to him to his friends as "my attaché of legation;" nor did he lessen that gentleman's dignity by telling any one that the attaché's salary was to be five hundred dollars a year. His own salary was only fifteen hundred dollars; and though his brother-in-law, Senator Rainsford, tried his best to get the amount raised, he was unsuccessful. The consulship to Opeki was instituted early in the '50's, to get rid of and reward a third or fourth cousin of the President's, whose services during the campaign were important, but whose after-presence was embarrassing. He had been created consul to Opeki as being more distant and unaccessible than any other known spot, and had lived and died there; and so little was known of the island, and so difficult was communication with it, that no one knew he was dead, until Captain Travis, in his hungry haste for office, had uprooted the sad fact. Captain Travis, as well as Albert, had a secondary reason for wishing to visit Opeki. His physician had told him to go to some warm climate for his rheumatism, and in accepting the consulship his object was rather to follow out his doctor's orders at his country's expense, than to serve his country at the expense of his rheumatism.

Albert could learn but very little of Opeki; nothing, indeed, but that it was situated about one hundred miles from the Island of Octavia, which island, in turn, was simply described as a coaling-station three hundred miles distant from the coast of California. Steamers from San Francisco to Yokohama stopped every third week at Octavia, and that was all that either Captain Travis or his secretary could learn of their new home. This was so very little, that Albert stipulated to stay only as long as he liked it, and to return to the States within a few months if he found such a change of plan desirable.

As he was going to what was an almost undiscovered country, he thought it would be advisable to furnish himself with a supply of articles with which he might trade with the native Opekians, and for this purpose he purchased a large quantity of brass rods, because he had read that Stanley did so, and added to these, brass curtain chains and about two hundred leaden medals similar to those sold by street pedlers during the Constitutional Centennial celebration in New York City.

He also collected even more beautiful but less expensive decorations for Christmas trees, at a wholesale house on Park Row. These he hoped to exchange for furs or feathers or weapons, or for whatever other curious and valuable trophies the Island of Opeki boasted. He already pictured his rooms on his return hung fantastically with crossed spears and boomerangs, feather head-dresses, and ugly idols.

His friends told him that he was doing a very foolish thing, and argued that once out of the newspaper world, it would be hard to regain his place in it. But he thought the novel that he would write while lost to the world at Opeki would serve to make up for his temporary absence from it, and he expressly and impressively stipulated that the editor should wire him if there was a war.

Captain Travis and his secretary crossed the continent without adventure, and took passage from San Francisco on the first steamer that touched at Octavia. They reached that island in three days, and learned with some concern that there was no regular communication with Opeki, and that it would be necessary to charter a sailboat for the trip. Two fishermen agreed to take them and their trunks, and to get them to their destination within sixteen hours if the wind held good. It was a most unpleasant sail. The rain fell with calm, relentless persistence from what was apparently a clear sky; the wind tossed the waves as high as the mast and made Captain Travis ill; and as there was no deck to the big boat, they were forced to huddle up under pieces of canvas, and talked but little. Captain Travis complained of frequent twinges of rheumatism, and gazed forlornly over the gunwale at the empty waste of water.

"If I've got to serve a term of imprisonment on a rock in the middle of the ocean for four years," he said, "I might just as well have done something first to deserve it. This is a pretty way to treat a man who bled for his country. This is gratitude, this is." Albert pulled heavily on his pipe, and wiped the rain and spray from his face and smiled.

"Oh, it won't be so bad when we get there," he said; "they say these Southern people are always hospitable, and the whites will be glad to see any one from the States."

"There will be a round of diplomatic dinners," said the consul, with an attempt at cheerfulness. "I have brought two uniforms to wear at them."

It was seven o'clock in the evening when the rain ceased, and one of the black, half-naked fishermen nodded and pointed at a little low line on the horizon.

"Opeki," he said. The line grew in length until it proved to be an island with great mountains rising to the clouds, and as they drew nearer and nearer, showed a level coast running back to the foot of the mountains and covered with a forest of palms. They next made out a village of thatched huts around a grassy square, and at some distance from the village a wooden structure with a tin roof.

"I wonder where the town is," asked the consul, with a nervous glance at the fishermen. One of them told him that what he saw was the town.

"That?" gasped the consul. "Is that where all the people on the island live?"

The fisherman nodded; but the other added that there were other natives further back in the mountains, but that they were bad men who fought and ate each other. The consul and his attaché of legation gazed at the mountains with unspoken misgivings. They were quite near now, and could see an immense crowd of men and women, all of them black, and clad but in the simplest garments, waiting to receive them. They seemed greatly excited and ran in and out of the huts, and up and down the beach, as wildly as so many black ants. But in the front of the group they distinguished three men who they could see were white, though they were clothed, like the others, simply in a shirt and a short pair of trousers. Two of these three suddenly sprang away on a run and disappeared among the palm-trees; but the third one, when he recognized the American flag in the halyards, threw his straw hat in the water and began turning handsprings over the sand.

"That young gentleman, at least," said Albert, gravely, "seems pleased to see us."

A dozen of the natives sprang into the water and came wading and swimming towards them, grinning and shouting and swinging their arms.

"I don't think it's quite safe, do you?" said the consul, looking out wildly to the open sea. "You see, they don't know who I am."

A great black giant threw one arm over the gunwale and shouted something that sounded as if it were spelt Owah, Owah, as the boat carried him through the surf.

"How do you do?" said Gordon, doubtfully. The boat shook the giant off under the wave and beached itself so suddenly that the American consul was thrown forward to his knees. Gordon did not wait to pick him up, but jumped out and shook hands with the young man who had turned handsprings, while the natives gathered about them in a circle and chatted and laughed in delighted excitement.

"I'm awful glad to see you," said the young man, eagerly. "My name's Stedman. I'm from New Haven, Connecticut. Where are you from?"

"New York," said Albert. "This," he added, pointing solemnly to Captain Travis, who was still on his knees in the boat, "is the American consul to Opeki." The American consul to Opeki gave a wild look at Mr. Stedman of New Haven and at the natives.

"See here, young man," he gasped, "is this all there is of Opeki?"

"The American consul?" said young Stedman, with a gasp of amazement, and looking from Albert to Captain Travis. "Why, I never supposed they would send another here; the last one died about fifteen years ago, and there hasn't been one since. I've been living in the consul's office with the Bradleys, but I'll move out, of course. I'm sure I'm awfully glad to see you. It'll make it so much more pleasant for me."

"Yes," said Captain Travis, bitterly, as he lifted his rheumatic leg over the boat; "that's why we came."

Mr. Stedman did not notice this. He was too much pleased to be anything but hospitable. "You are soaking wet, aren't you?" he said; "and hungry, I guess. You come right over to the consul's office and get on some other things."

He turned to the natives and gave some rapid orders in their language, and some of them jumped into the boat at this, and began to lift out the trunks, and others ran off towards a large, stout old native, who was sitting gravely on a log, smoking, with the rain beating unnoticed on his gray hair.

"They've gone to tell the King," said Stedman; "but you'd better get something to eat first, and then I'll be happy to present you properly."

"The King," said Captain Travis, with some awe; "is there a king?"

"I never saw a king," Gordon remarked, "and I'm sure I never expected to see one sitting on a log in the rain."

"He's a very good king," said Stedman, confidentially; "and though you mightn't think it to look at him, he's a terrible stickler for etiquette and form. After supper he'll give you an audience; and if you have any tobacco, you had better give him some as a present, and you'd better say it's from the President: he doesn't like to take presents from common people, he's so proud. The only reason he borrows mine is because he thinks I'm the President's son."

"What makes him think that?" demanded the consul, with some shortness. Young Mr. Stedman looked nervously at the consul and at Albert, and said that he guessed some one must have told him.

The consul's office was divided into four rooms with an open court in the middle, filled with palms, and watered somewhat unnecessarily by a fountain.

"I made that," said Stedman, in a modest offhand way. "I made it out of hollow bamboo reeds connected with a spring. And now I'm making one for the King. He saw this and had a lot of bamboo sticks put up all over the town, without any underground connections, and couldn't make out why the water wouldn't spurt out of them. And because mine spurts, he thinks I'm a magician."

"I suppose," grumbled the consul, "some one told him that too."

"I suppose so," said Mr. Stedman, uneasily.

There was a veranda around the consul's office, and inside the walls were hung with skins, and pictures from illustrated papers, and there was a good deal of bamboo furniture, and four broad, cool-looking beds. The place was as clean as a kitchen. "I made the furniture," said Stedman, "and the Bradleys keep the place in order."

"Who are the Bradleys?" asked Albert.

"The Bradleys are those two men you saw with me," said Stedman; "they deserted from a British man-of-war that stopped here for coal, and they act as my servants. One is Bradley, Sr., and the other, Bradley, Jr."

"Then vessels do stop here occasionally?" the consul said, with a pleased smile.

"Well, not often," said Stedman. "Not so very often; about once a year. The *Nelson* thought this was Octavia, and put off again as soon as she found out her mistake, but the Bradleys took to the bush, and the boat's crew couldn't find them. When they saw your flag, they thought you might mean to send them back, so they ran off to hide again: they'll be back, though, when they get hungry."

The supper young Stedman spread for his guests, as he still treated them, was very refreshing and very good. There was cold fish and pigeon pie, and a hot omelet filled with mushrooms and olives and tomatoes and onions all sliced up together, and strong black coffee. After supper, Stedman went off to see the King, and came back in a little while to say that his Majesty would give them an audience the next day after breakfast. "It is too dark now," Stedman explained; "and it's raining so that they can't make the street lamps burn. Did you happen to notice our lamps? I invented them; but they don't work very well yet. I've got the right idea, though, and I'll soon have the town illuminated all over, whether it rains or not."

The consul had been very silent and indifferent, during supper, to all around him. Now he looked up with some show of interest.

"How much longer is it going to rain, do you think?" he asked.

"Oh, I don't know," said Stedman, critically. "Not more than two months, I should say." The consul rubbed his rheumatic leg and sighed, but said nothing.

The Bradleys returned about ten o'clock, and came in very sheepishly. The consul had gone off to pay the boatmen who had brought them, and Albert in his absence assured the sailor's that there was not the least danger of their being sent away. Then he turned into one of the beds, and Stedman took one in another room, leaving the room he had occupied heretofore for the consul. As he was saying good-night, Albert suggested that he had not yet told them how he came to be on a deserted island; but Stedman only laughed and said that that was a long story, and that he would tell him all about it in the morning. So Albert went off to bed without waiting for the consul to return, and fell asleep, wondering at the strangeness of his new life, and assuring himself that if the rain only kept up, he would have his novel finished in a month.

The sun was shining brightly when he awoke, and the palm-trees outside were nodding gracefully in a warm breeze. From the court came the odor of strange flowers, and from the window he could see the ocean brilliantly blue, and with the sun coloring the spray that beat against the coral reefs on the shore.

"Well, the consul can't complain of this," he said, with a laugh of satisfaction; and pulling on a bathrobe, he stepped into the next room to awaken Captain Travis. But the room was quite empty, and the bed undisturbed. The consul's trunk remained just where it had been placed near the door, and on it lay a large sheet of foolscap, with writing on it, and addressed at the top to Albert Gordon. The handwriting was the consul's. Albert picked it up and read it with much anxiety. It began abruptly:—

"The fishermen who brought us to this forsaken spot tell me that it rains here six months in the year, and that this is the first month. I came here to serve my country, for which I fought and bled, but I did not come here to die of rheumatism and pneumonia. I can serve my country better by staying alive; and whether it rains or not, I don't like it. I have been grossly deceived, and I am going back. Indeed, by the time you get this, I will be on my return trip, as I intend leaving with the men who brought us here as soon as they can get the sail up. My cousin, Senator Rainsford, can fix it all right with the President, and can have me recalled in proper form after I get back. But of course it would not do for me to leave my post with no one to take my place, and no one could be more ably fitted to do so than yourself; so I feel no compunctions at leaving you behind. I hereby, therefore, accordingly appoint you my substitute with full power to act, to collect all fees, sign all papers, and attend to all matters pertaining to your office as American consul, and I trust you will worthily uphold the name of that country and government which it has always been my pleasure and duty to serve.

"Your sincere friend and superior officer,

"Leonard T. Travis.

"P.S. I did not care to disturb you by moving my trunk, so I left it, and you can make what use you please of whatever it contains, as I shall not want tropical garments where I am going. What you will need most, I think, is a waterproof and umbrella.

"P.S. Look out for that young man Stedman. He is too inventive. I hope you will like your high office; but as for myself, I am satisfied with little old New York. Opeki is just a bit too far from civilization to suit me."

Albert held the letter before him and read it over again before he moved. Then he jumped to the window. The boat was gone, and there was not a sign of it on the horizon.

"The miserable old hypocrite!" he cried, half angry and half laughing. "If he thinks I am going to stay here alone he is very greatly mistaken. And yet, why not?" he asked. He stopped soliloquizing and looked around him, thinking rapidly. As he stood there, Stedman came in from the other room, fresh and smiling from his morning's bath.

"Good morning," he said, "where's the consul?"

"The consul," said Albert, gravely, "is before you. In me you see the American consul to Opeki.

"Captain Travis," Albert explained, "has returned to the

United States. I suppose he feels that he can best serve his country by remaining on the spot. In case of another war, now, for instance, he would be there to save it again."

"And what are you going to do?" asked Stedman, anxiously. "You will not run away too, will you?"

Albert said that he intended to remain where he was and perform his consular duties, to appoint him his secretary, and to elevate the United States in the opinion of the Opekians above all other nations.

"They may not think much of the United States in England," he said; "but we are going to teach the people of Opeki that America is first on the map, and that there is no second."

"I'm sure it's very good of you to make me your secretary," said Stedman, with some pride. "I hope I won't make any mistakes. What are the duties of a consul's secretary?"

"That," said Albert, "I do not know. But you are rather good at inventing, so you can invent a few. That should be your first duty and you should attend to it at once. I will have trouble enough finding work for myself. Your salary is five hundred dollars a year; and now," he continued, briskly, "we want to prepare for this reception. We can tell the King that Travis was just a guard of honor for the trip, and that I have sent him back to tell the President of my safe arrival. That will keep the President from getting anxious. There is nothing," continued Albert, "like a uniform to impress people who live in the tropics, and Travis, it so happens, has two in his trunk. He intended to wear them on State occasions, and as I inherit the trunk and all that is in it, I intend to wear one of the uniforms, and you can have the other. But I have first choice, because I am consul."

Captain Travis's consular outfit consisted of one full dress and one undress United States uniform. Albert put on the dresscoat over a pair of white flannel trousers, and looked remarkably brave and handsome. Stedman, who was only eighteen and quite thin, did not appear so well, until Albert suggested his padding out his chest and shoulders with towels. This made him rather warm, but helped his general appearance.

"The two Bradleys must dress up, too," said Albert. "I think they ought to act as a guard of honor, don't you? The only things I have are blazers and jerseys; but it doesn't much matter what they wear, as long as they dress alike."

He accordingly called in the two Bradleys, and gave them each a pair of the captain's rejected white duck trousers, and a blue jersey apiece, with a big white Y on it.

"The students of Yale gave me that," he said to the younger Bradley, "in which to play football, and a great man gave me the other. His name is Walter Camp; and if you rip or soil that jersey, I'll send you back to England in irons; so be careful."

Stedman gazed at his companions in their different costumes, doubtfully. "It reminds me," he said, "of private theatricals. Of the time our church choir played 'Pinafore.'"

"Yes," assented Albert; "but I don't think we look quite gay enough. I tell you what we need—medals. You never saw a diplomat without a lot of decorations and medals."

"Well, I can fix that," Stedman said. "I've got a trunk-full. I used to be the fastest bicycle-rider in Connecticut, and I've got all my prizes with me."

Albert said doubtfully that that wasn't exactly the sort of medal he meant.

"Perhaps not," returned Stedman, as he began fumbling in his trunk; "but the King won't know the difference. He couldn't tell a cross of the Legion of Honor from a medal for the tug of war."

So the bicycle medals, of which Stedman seemed to have an innumerable quantity, were strung in profusion over Albert's uniform, and in a lesser quantity over Stedman's; while a handful of leaden ones, those sold on the streets for the Constitutional Centennial, with which Albert had provided himself, were wrapped up in a red silk handkerchief for presentation to the King: with them

Albert placed a number of brass rods and brass chains, much to Stedman's delighted approval.

"That is a very good idea," he said. "Democratic simplicity is the right thing at home, of course; but when you go abroad and mix with crowned heads, you want to show them that you know what's what."

"Well," said Albert, gravely, "I sincerely hope this crowned head don't know what's what. If he reads 'Connecticut Agricultural State Fair. One mile bicycle race. First Prize,' on this badge, when we are trying to make him believe it's a war medal, it may hurt his feelings."

Bradley, Jr., went ahead to announce the approach of the American embassy, which he did with so much manner that the King deferred the audience a half-hour, in order that he might better prepare to receive his visitors. When the audience did take place, it attracted the entire population to the green spot in front of the King's palace, and their delight and excitement over the appearance of the visitors was sincere and hearty. The King was too polite to appear much surprised, but he showed his delight over his presents as simply and openly as a child. Thrice he insisted on embracing Albert, and kissing him three times on the forehead, which, Stedman assured him in a side whisper, was a great honor; an honor which was not extended to the secretary, although he was given a necklace of animals' claws instead, with which he was better satisfied.

After this reception, the embassy marched back to the consul's office, surrounded by an immense number of the natives, some of whom ran ahead and looked back at them, and crowded so close that the two Bradleys had to poke at those nearest with their guns. The crowd remained outside the office even after the procession of four had disappeared, and cheered. This suggested to Gordon that this would be a good time to make a speech, which he accordingly did, Stedman translating it, sentence by sentence. At the conclusion of this effort, Albert distributed a number of brass rings among the married men present, which they placed on whichever finger fitted best, and departed delighted.

Albert had wished to give the rings to the married women, but Stedman pointed out to him that it would be much cheaper to give them to the married men; for while one woman could only have one husband, one man could have at least six wives.

"And now, Stedman," said Albert, after the mob had gone, "tell me what you are doing on this island."

"It's a very simple story," Stedman said. "I am the representative, or agent, or operator, for the Yokohama Cable Company. The Yokohama Cable Company is a company organized in San Francisco, for the purpose of laying a cable to Yokohama. It is a stock company; and though it started out very well, the stock has fallen very low. Between ourselves, it is not worth over three or four cents. When the officers of the company found out that no one would buy their stock, and that no one believed in them or their scheme, they laid a cable to Octavia, and extended it on to this island. Then they said they had run out of ready money, and would wait until they got more before laying their cable any further. I do not think they ever will lay it any further, but that is none of my business. My business is to answer cable messages from San Francisco, so that the people who visit the home office can see that at least a part of the cable is working. That sometimes impresses them, and they buy stock. There is another chap over in Octavia, who relays all my messages and all my replies to those messages that come to me through him from San Francisco. They never send a message unless they have brought some one to the office whom they want to impress, and who, they think, has money to invest in the Y.C.C. stock, and so we never go near the wire, except at three o'clock every afternoon. And then generally only to say 'How are you?' or 'It's raining,' or something like that. I've been saying 'It's raining' now for the last three months, but today I will say that the new consul has arrived. That will be a pleasant surprise for the chap in Octavia, for he must be tired hearing about the weather. He generally answers, 'Here too,' or 'So you said,' or something like that. I don't know what he says to the home office. He's brighter than I am, and that's why they put him between the two ends. He can see that the messages are transmitted more fully and more correctly, in a way to please possible subscribers."

"Sort of copy editor," suggested Albert.

"Yes, something of that sort, I fancy," said Stedman.

They walked down to the little shed on the shore, where the Y.C.C. office was placed, at three that day, and Albert watched Stedman send off his message with much interest. The "chap at Octavia," on being informed that the American consul had arrived at Opeki, inquired, somewhat disrespectfully, "Is it a life sentence?"

"What does he mean by that?" asked Albert.

"I suppose," said his secretary, doubtfully, "that he thinks it a sort of a punishment to be sent to Opeki. I hope you won't grow to think so."

"Opeki is all very well," said Gordon, "or it will be when we get things going our way."

As they walked back to the office, Albert noticed a brass cannon, perched on a rock at the entrance to the harbor. This had been put there by the last consul, but it had not been fired for many years. Albert immediately ordered the two Bradleys to get it in order, and to rig up a flagpole beside it, for one of his American flags, which they were to salute every night when they lowered it at sundown.

"And when we are not using it," he said, "the King can borrow it to celebrate with, if he doesn't impose on us too often. The royal salute ought to be twenty-one guns, I think; but that would use up too much powder, so he will have to content himself with two."

"Did you notice," asked Stedman that night, as they sat on the veranda of the consul's house, in the moonlight, "how the people bowed to us as we passed?"

"Yes," Albert said he had noticed it. "Why?"

"Well, they never saluted me," replied Stedman. "That sign of respect is due to the show we made at the reception."

"It is due to us, in any event," said the consul, severely. "I tell you, my secretary, that we, as the representatives of the United States government, must be properly honored on this island. We must become a power. And we must do so without getting into trouble with the King. We must make them honor him, too, and then as we push him up, we will push ourselves up at the same time."

"They don't think much of consuls in Opeki," said Stedman, doubtfully. "You see the last one was a pretty poor sort. He brought the office into disrepute, and it wasn't really until I came and told them what a fine country the United States was, that they had any opinion of it at all. Now we must change all that."

"That is just what we will do," said Albert. "We will transform Opeki into a powerful and beautiful city. We will make these people work. They must put up a palace for the King, and lay out streets, and build wharves, and drain the town properly, and light it. I haven't seen this patent lighting apparatus of yours, but you had better get to work at it at once, and I'll persuade the King to appoint you commissioner of highways and gas, with authority to make his people toil. And I," he cried, in free enthusiasm, "will organize a navy and a standing army. Only," he added, with a relapse of interest, "there isn't anybody to fight."

"There isn't?" said Stedman, grimly, with a scornful smile. "You just go hunt up old Messenwah and the Hillmen with your standing army once, and you'll get all the fighting you want."

"The Hillmen?" said Albert.

"The Hillmen are the natives that live up there in the hills," Stedman said, nodding his head towards the three high mountains at the other end of the island, that stood out blackly against the purple, moonlit sky. "There are nearly as many of them as there are Opekians, and they hunt and fight for a living and for the pleasure of it. They have an old rascal named Messenwah for a king, and they come down here about once every three months, and tear things up."

Albert sprang to his feet.

"Oh, they do, do they?" he said, staring up at the mountain tops. "They come down here and tear up things, do they? Well, I think we'll stop that, I think we'll stop that! I don't care how many there are. I'll get the two Bradleys to tell me all they know about drilling, tomorrow morning, and we'll drill these Opekians, and have sham battles, and attacks, and repulses, until I make a lot of wild, howling Zulus out of them. And when the Hillmen come down to pay their quarterly visit, they'll go back again on a run. At least some of them will," he added ferociously. "Some of them will stay right here."

"Dear me, dear me!" said Stedman, with awe; "you are a born fighter, aren't you?"

"Well, you wait and see," said Gordon; "may be I am. I haven't studied tactics of war and the history of battles, so that I might be a great war correspondent, without learning something. And there is only one king on this island, and that is old Ollypybus himself. And I'll go over and have a talk with him about it tomorrow."

Young Stedman walked up and down the length of the veranda, in and out of the moonlight, with his hands in his pockets, and his head on his chest. "You have me all stirred up, Gordon," he said; "you seem so confident and bold, and you're not so much older than I am, either."

"My training has been different; that's all," said the reporter.

"Yes," Stedman said bitterly; "I have been sitting in an office ever since I left school, sending news over a wire or a cable, and you have been out in the world, gathering it."

"And now," said Gordon, smiling, and putting his arm around the other boy's shoulders, "we are going to make news ourselves."

"There is one thing I want to say to you before you turn in," said Stedman. "Before you suggest all these improvements on Ollypybus, you must remember that he has ruled absolutely here for twenty years, and that he does not think much of consuls. He has only seen your predecessor and yourself. He likes you because you appeared with such dignity, and because of the presents; but if I were you, I wouldn't suggest these improvements as coming from yourself."

"I don't understand," said Gordon; "who could they come from?"

"Well," said Stedman, "if you will allow me to advise—and you see I know these people pretty well—I would have all these suggestions come from the President direct."

"The President!" exclaimed Gordon; "but how? what does the President know or care about Opeki? and it would take so long—oh, I see, the cable. Is that what you have been doing?" he asked.

"Well, only once," said Stedman, guiltily; "that was when he wanted to turn me out of the consul's office, and I had a cable that very afternoon, from the President, ordering me to stay where I was. Ollypybus doesn't understand the cable, of course, but he knows that it sends messages; and sometimes I pretend to send messages for him to the President; but he began asking me to tell the President to come and pay him a visit, and I had to stop it."

"I'm glad you told me," said Gordon. "The President shall begin to cable tomorrow. He will need an extra appropriation from Congress to pay for his private cablegrams alone."

"And there's another thing," said Stedman. "In all your plans, you've arranged for the people's improvement, but not for their amusement; and they are a peaceful, jolly, simple sort of people, and we must please them."

"Have they no games or amusements of their own?" asked Gordon.

"Well, not what we would call games."

"Very well, then, I'll teach them baseball. Football would be too warm. But that plaza in front of the King's bungalow, where his palace is going to be, is just the place for a diamond. On the whole, though," added the consul, after a moment's reflection, "you'd better attend to that yourself. I don't think it becomes my dignity as American consul to take off my coat and give lessons to young Opekians in sliding to bases; do you? No; I think you'd better do that. The Bradleys will help you, and you had better begin tomorrow. You have been wanting to know what a secretary of legation's duties are, and now you know. It's to organize baseball nines. And after you get yours ready," he added, as he turned into his room for the night, "I'll train one that will sweep yours off the face of the island. For *this* American consul can pitch three curves."

The best-laid plans of men go far astray, sometimes, and the great and beautiful city that was to rise on the coast of Opeki was not built in a day. Nor was it ever built. For before the Bradleys could mark out the foul-lines for the baseball field on the plaza, or teach their standing army the goose step, or lay bamboo pipes for the watermains, or clear away the cactus for the extension of the King's palace, the Hillmen paid Opeki their quarterly visit.

Albert had called on the King the next morning, with Stedman as his interpreter, as he had said he would, and, with maps and sketches, had shown his Majesty what he proposed to do towards improving Opeki and ennobling her king, and when the King saw Albert's freehand sketches of wharves with tall ships lying at anchor, and rows of Opekian warriors with the Bradleys at their head, and the design for his new palace, and a royal sedan-chair, he believed that these things were already his, and not still only on paper, and he appointed Albert his Minister of War, Stedman his Minister of Home Affairs, and selected two of his wisest and oldest subjects to serve them as joint advisers. His enthusiasm was even greater than Gordon's, because he did not appreciate the difficulties. He thought Gordon a semi-god, a worker of miracles, and urged the putting up of a monument to him at once in the public plaza, to which Albert objected, on the ground that it would be too suggestive of an idol; and to which Stedman also objected, but for the less unselfish reason that it would "be in the way of the pitcher's box."

They were feverishly discussing all these great changes, and Stedman was translating as rapidly as he could translate, the speeches of four different men—for the two counsellors had been called in, all of whom wanted to speak at once—when there came from outside a great shout, and the screams of women, and the clashing of iron, and the pattering footsteps of men running.

As they looked at one another in startled surprise, a native ran into the room, followed by Bradley, Jr., and threw himself down before the King. While he talked, beating his hands and bowing before Ollypybus, Bradley, Jr., pulled his forelock to the consul, and told how this man lived on the far outskirts of the village; how he had been captured while out hunting, by a number of the Hillmen; and how he had escaped to tell the people that their old enemies were on the war path again, and rapidly approaching the village.

Outside, the women were gathering in the plaza, with the children about them, and the men were running from hut to hut, warning their fellows, and arming themselves with spears and swords, and the native bows and arrows.

"They might have waited until we had that army trained," said Gordon, in a tone of the keenest displeasure. "Tell me, quick, what do they generally do when they come?"

"Steal all the cattle and goats, and a woman or two, and set fire to the huts in the outskirts," replied Stedman.

"Well, we must stop them," said Gordon, jumping up. "We must take out a flag of truce and treat with them. They must be kept off until I have my army in working order. It is most inconvenient. If they had only waited two months, now, or six weeks even, we could have done something; but now we must make peace. Tell the King we are going out to fix things with them, and tell him to keep off his warriors until he learns whether we succeed or fail."

"But, Gordon!" gasped Stedman. "Albert! You don't understand. Why, man, this isn't a street fight or a cane rush. They'll stick you full of spears, dance on your body, and eat you, maybe. A flag of truce!—you're talking nonsense. What do they know of a flag of truce?"

"You're talking nonsense, too," said Albert, "and you're talking to your superior officer. If you are not with me in this, go back to your cable, and tell the man in Octavia that it's a warm day, and that the sun is shining; but if you've any spirit in you—and I think you have—run to the office and get my Winchester rifles, and the two shot guns, and my revolvers, and my uniform, and a lot of brass things for presents, and run all the way there and back. And make time. Play you're riding a bicycle at the Agricultural Fair."

Stedman did not hear this last; for he was already off and away, pushing through the crowd, and calling on Bradley, Sr., to follow him. Bradley, Jr., looked at Gordon with eyes that snapped, like a dog that is waiting for his master to throw a stone.

"I can fire a Winchester, sir," he said. "Old Tom can't. He's no good at long range 'cept with a big gun, sir. Don't give him the Winchester. Give it to me, please, sir."

Albert met Stedman in the plaza, and pulled off his blazer, and put on Captain Travis's—now his—uniform coat, and his white pith helmet.

"Now, Jack," he said, "get up there and tell these people that we are going out to make peace with these Hillmen, or bring them back prisoners of war. Tell them we are the preservers of their homes and wives and children; and you, Bradley, take these presents, and young Bradley, keep close to me, and carry this rifle."

Stedman's speech was hot and wild enough to suit a critical and feverish audience before a barricade in Paris. And when he was through, Gordon and Bradley punctuated his oration by firing off the two Winchester rifles in the air, at which the people jumped and fell on their knees, and prayed to their several gods. The fighting men of the village followed the four white men to the out-skirts, and took up their stand there as Stedman told them to do, and the four walked on over the roughly hewn road, to meet the enemy.

Gordon walked with Bradley, Jr., in advance. Stedman and old Tom Bradley followed close behind, with the two shotguns, and the presents in a basket.

"Are these Hillmen used to guns?" asked Gordon. Stedman said no, they were not.

"This shotgun of mine is the only one on the island," he explained, "and we never came near enough them, before, to do anything with it. It only carries a hundred yards. The Opekians never make any show of resistance. They are quite content if the Hillmen satisfy themselves with the outlying huts, as long as they leave them and the town alone; so they seldom come to close quarters."

The four men walked on for a half an hour or so, in silence, peering eagerly on every side; but it was not until they had left the woods and marched out into the level stretch of grassy country, that they came upon the enemy. The Hillmen were about forty in number, and were as savage and ugly-looking giants as any in a picture book. They had captured a dozen cows and goats, and were driving them on before them, as they advanced further upon the village. When they saw the four men, they gave a mixed chorus of cries and yells, and some of them stopped, and others ran forward, shaking their spears, and shooting their broad arrows into the ground before them. A tall, gray-bearded, muscular old man, with a skirt of feathers about him, and necklaces of bones and animals' claws around his bare chest, ran in front of them, and seemed to be trying to make them approach more slowly.

"Is that Messenwah?" asked Gordon.

"Yes," said Stedman; "he is trying to keep them back. I don't believe he ever saw a white man before."

"Stedman," said Albert, speaking quickly, "give your gun to Bradley, and go forward with your arms in the air, and waving your handkerchief, and tell them in their language that the King is coming. If they go at you, Bradley and I will kill a goat or two, to show them what we can do with the rifles; and if that don't stop them, we will shoot at their legs; and if that don't stop them—I guess you'd better come back, and we'll all run."

Stedman looked at Albert, and Albert looked at Stedman, and neither of them winced or flinched.

"Is this another of my secretary's duties?" asked the younger boy.

"Yes," said the consul; "but a resignation is always in order. You needn't go if you don't like it. You see, you know the language and I don't, but I know how to shoot, and you don't."

"That's perfectly satisfactory," said Stedman, handing his gun to old Bradley. "I only wanted to know why I was to be sacrificed, instead of one of the Bradleys. It's because I know the language. Bradley, Sr., you see the evil results of a higher education. Wish me luck, please," he said, "and for goodness' sake," he added impressively, "don't waste much time shooting goats."

The Hillmen had stopped about two hundred yards off, and were drawn up in two lines, shouting, and dancing, and hurling taunting remarks at their few adversaries. The stolen cattle were bunched together back of the King. As Stedman walked steadily forward with his handkerchief fluttering, and howling out something in their own tongue, they stopped and listened. As he advanced, his three companions followed him at about fifty yards in the rear. He was one hundred and fifty yards from the Hillmen, before they made out what he said, and then one of the young braves, resenting it as an insult to his chief, shot an arrow at him. Stedman dodged the arrow, and stood his ground without even taking a step backwards, only turning slightly to put his hands to his mouth, and to shout something which sounded to his companions like, "About time to begin on the goats." But the instant the young man had fired, King Messenwah swung his club and knocked him down, and none of the others moved. Then Messenwah advanced before his men to meet Stedman, and on Stedman's opening and shutting his hands to show that he was unarmed, the King threw down his club and spears, and came forward as empty-handed as himself.

"Ah," gasped Bradley, Jr., with his finger trembling on his lever, "let me take a shot at him now." Gordon struck the man's gun up, and walked forward in all the glory of his gold and blue uniform; for both he and Stedman saw now that Messenwah was more impressed by their appearance, and in the fact that they were white men, than with any threats of immediate war. So when he saluted Gordon haughtily, that young man gave him a haughty nod in return, and bade Stedman tell the King that he would permit him to sit down. The King did not quite appear to like this, but he sat down, nevertheless, and nodded his head gravely.

"Now tell him," said Gordon, "that I come from the ruler of the greatest nation on earth, and that I recognize Ollypybus as the only King of this island, and that I come to this little three-penny King with either peace and presents, or bullets and war."

"Have I got to tell him he's a little three-penny King?" said Stedman, plaintively.

"No; you needn't give a literal translation; it can be as free as you please."

"Thanks," said the secretary, humbly.

"And tell him," continued Gordon, "that we will give presents to him and his warriors if he keeps away from Ollypybus, and agrees to keep away always. If he won't do that, try to get him to agree to stay away for three months at least, and by that time we can get word to San Francisco, and have a dozen muskets over here in two months; and when our time of probation is up, and he and his merry men come dancing down the hillside, we will blow them up as high as his mountains. But you needn't tell him that, either. And if he is proud and haughty, and would rather fight, ask him to restrain himself until we show what we can do with our weapons at two hundred yards."

Stedman seated himself in the long grass in front of the King, and with many revolving gestures of his arms, and much pointing at Gordon, and profound nods and bows, retold what Gordon had dictated. When he had finished, the King looked at the bundle of presents, and at the guns, of which Stedman had given a very wonderful account, but answered nothing.

"I guess," said Stedman, with a sigh, "that we will have to give him a little practical demonstration to help matters. I am sorry, but I think one of those goats has got to die. It's like vivisection. The lower order of animals have to suffer for the good of the higher."

"Oh," said Bradley, Jr., cheerfully, "I'd just as soon shoot one of those niggers as one of the goats."

So Stedman bade the King tell his men to drive a goat towards them, and the King did so, and one of the men struck one of the goats with his spear, and it ran clumsily across the plain.

"Take your time, Bradley," said Gordon. "Aim low, and if you hit it, you can have it for supper."

"And if you miss it," said Stedman, gloomily, "Messenwah may have us for supper."

The Hillmen had seated themselves a hundred yards off, while the leaders were debating, and they now rose curiously and watched Bradley, as he sank upon one knee, and covered the goat with his rifle. When it was about one hundred and fifty yards off, he fired, and the goat fell over dead.

And then all the Hillmen, with the King himself, broke away on a run, towards the dead animal, with much shouting. The King came back alone, leaving his people standing about and examining the goat. He was much excited, and talked and gesticulated violently.

"He says—" said Stedman; "he says—"

"What? yes; go on."

"He says—goodness me!—what do you think he says?"

"Well, what does he say?" cried Gordon, in great excitement. "Don't keep it all to yourself."

"He says," said Stedman, "that we are deceived. That he is no longer King of the Island of Opeki, that he is in great fear of us, and that he has got himself into no end of trouble. He says he sees that we are indeed mighty men, that to us he is as helpless as the wild boar before the javelin of the hunter."

"Well, he's right," said Gordon. "Go on."

"But that which we ask is no longer his to give. He has sold his kingship and his right to this island to another king, who came to him two days ago in a great canoe, and who made noises as we do—with guns, I suppose he means—and to whom he sold the island for a watch that he has in a bag around his neck. And that he signed a paper, and made marks on a piece of bark, to show that he gave up the island freely and forever."

"What does he mean?" said Gordon. "How can he give up the island? Ollypybus is the king of half of it, anyway, and he knows it."

"That's just it," said Stedman. "That's what frightens him. He said he didn't care about Ollypybus, and didn't count him in when he made the treaty, because he is such a peaceful chap that he knew he could thrash him into doing anything he wanted him to do. And now that you have turned up and taken Ollypybus's part, he wishes he hadn't sold the island, and wishes to know if you are angry."

"Angry? of course I'm angry," said Gordon, glaring as grimly at the frightened monarch as he thought was safe. "Who wouldn't be angry? Who do you think these people were who made a fool of him, Stedman? Ask him to let us see this watch."

Stedman did so, and the King fumbled among his necklaces

until he had brought out a leather bag tied round his neck with a cord, and containing a plain stem-winding silver watch marked on the inside "Munich."

"That doesn't tell anything," said Gordon. "But it's plain enough. Some foreign ship of war has settled on this place as a coaling-station, or has annexed it for colonization, and they've sent a boat ashore, and they've made a treaty with this old chap, and forced him to sell his birthright for a mess of porridge. Now, that's just like those monarchical pirates, imposing upon a poor old black."

Old Bradley looked at him impudently.

"Not at all," said Gordon; "it's quite different with us; we don't want to rob him or Ollypybus, or to annex their land. All we want to do is to improve it, and have the fun of running it for them and meddling in their affairs of state. Well, Stedman," he said, "what shall we do?"

Stedman said that the best and only thing to do was to threaten to take the watch away from Messenwah, but to give him a revolver instead, which would make a friend of him for life, and to keep him supplied with cartridges only as long as he behaved himself, and then to make him understand that, as Ollypybus had not given his consent to the loss of the island, Messenwah's agreement, or treaty, or whatever it was, did not stand, and that he had better come down the next day, early in the morning, and join in a general consultation. This was done, and Messenwah agreed willingly to their proposition, and was given his revolver and shown how to shoot it, while the other presents were distributed among the other men, who were as happy over them as girls with a full dance-card.

"And now, tomorrow," said Stedman, "understand, you are all to come down unarmed, and sign a treaty with great Ollypybus, in which he will agree to keep to one half of the island, if you keep to yours, and there must be no more wars or goat stealing, or this gentleman on my right and I will come up and put holes in you just as the gentleman on the left did with the goat."

Messenwah and his warriors promised to come early, and saluted reverently as Gordon and his three companions walked up together very proudly and stiffly.

"Do you know how I feel?" said Gordon.

"How?" asked Stedman.

"I feel as I used to do in the city, when the boys in the street were throwing snowballs, and I had to go by with a high hat on my head and pretend not to know they were behind me. I always felt a cold chill down my spinal column, and I could feel that snowball, whether it came or not, right in the small of my back. And I can feel one of those men pulling his bow, now, and the arrow sticking out of my right shoulder."

"Oh, no, you can't," said Stedman. "They are too much afraid of those rifles. But I do feel sorry for any of those warriors whom old man Massenwah doesn't like, now that he has that revolver. He isn't the sort to practise on goats."

There was great rejoicing when Stedman and Gordon told their story to the King, and the people learned that they were not to have their huts burned and their cattle stolen. The armed Opekians formed a guard around the ambassadors and escorted them to their homes with cheers and shouts, and the women ran at their side and tried to kiss Gordon's hand.

"I'm sorry I can't speak the language, Stedman," said Gordon, "or I would tell them what a brave man you are. You are too modest to do it yourself, even if I dictated something for you to say. As for me," he said, pulling off his uniform, "I am thoroughly disgusted and disappointed. It never occurred to me until it was all over, that this was my chance to be a war correspondent. It wouldn't have been much of a war, but then I would have been the only one on the spot, and that counts for a great deal. Still, my time may come."

"We have a great deal on hand for tomorrow," said Gordon

that evening, "and we had better turn in early."

And so the people were still singing and rejoicing down in the village, when the two conspirators for the peace of the country went to sleep for the night. It seemed to Gordon as though he had hardly turned his pillow twice to get the coolest side, when some one touched him, and he saw, by the light of the dozen glow-worms in the tumbler by his bedside, a tall figure at its foot.

"It's me—Bradley," said the figure.

"Yes," said Gordon, with the haste of a man to show that sleep has no hold on him; "exactly; what is it?"

"There is a ship of war in the harbor," Bradley answered in a whisper. "I heard her anchor chains rattle when she came to, and that woke me. I could hear that if I were dead. And then I made sure by her lights; she's a great boat, sir, and I can know she's a ship of war by the challenging, when they change the watch. I thought you'd like to know, sir."

Gordon sat up and clutched his knees with his hands. "Yes, of course," he said; "you are quite right. Still, I don't see what there is to do."

He did not wish to show too much youthful interest, but though fresh from civilization, he had learned how far from it he was, and he was curious to see this sign of it that had come so much more quickly than he had anticipated.

"Wake Mr. Stedman, will you?" said he, "and we will go and take a look at her."

"You can see nothing but the lights," said Bradley, as he left the room; "it's a black night, sir."

Stedman was not new from the sight of men and ships of war, and came in half dressed and eager.

"Do you suppose it's the big canoe Messenwah spoke of?" he said.

"I thought of that," said Gordon.

The three men fumbled their way down the road to the plaza,

and saw, as soon as they turned into it, the great outlines and the brilliant lights of an immense vessel, still more immense in the darkness, and glowing like a strange monster of the sea, with just a suggestion here and there, where the lights spread, of her cabins and bridges. As they stood on the shore, shivering in the cool night wind, they heard the bells strike over the water.

"It's two o'clock," said Bradley, counting.

"Well, we can do nothing, and they cannot mean to do much tonight," Albert said. "We had better get some more sleep, and, Bradley, you keep watch and tell us as soon as day breaks."

"Aye, aye, sir," said the sailor.

"If that's the man-of-war that made the treaty with Messenwah, and Messenwah turns up tomorrow, it looks as if our day would be pretty well filled up," said Albert, as they felt their way back to the darkness.

"What do you intend to do?" asked his secretary, with a voice of some concern.

"I don't know," Albert answered gravely, from the blackness of the night. "It looks as if we were getting ahead just a little too fast; doesn't it? Well," he added, as they reached the house, "let's try to keep in step with the procession, even if we can't be drum-majors and walk in front of it." And with this cheering tone of confidence in their ears, the two diplomats went soundly asleep again.

The light of the rising sun filled the room, and the parrots were chattering outside, when Bradley woke him again.

"They are sending a boat ashore, sir," he said excitedly, and filled with the importance of the occasion. "She's a German man-of-war, and one of the new model. A beautiful boat, sir; for her lines were laid in Glasgow, and I can tell that, no matter what flag she flies. You had best be moving to meet them: the village isn't awake yet."

Albert took a cold bath and dressed leisurely; then he made

Bradley, Jr., who had slept through it all, get up breakfast, and the two young men ate it and drank their coffee comfortably and with an air of confidence that deceived their servants, if it did not deceive themselves. But when they came down the path, smoking and swinging their sticks, and turned into the plaza, their composure left them like a mask, and they stopped where they stood. The plaza was enclosed by the natives gathered in whispering groups, and depressed by fear and wonder. On one side were crowded all the Messenwah warriors, unarmed, and as silent and disturbed as the Opekians. In the middle of the plaza some twenty sailors were busy rearing and bracing a tall flag-staff that they had shaped from a royal palm, and they did this as unconcernedly and as contemptuously, and with as much indifference to the strange groups on either side of them, as though they were working on a barren coast, with nothing but the startled seagulls about them. As Albert and Stedman came upon the scene, the flagpole was in place, and the halliards hung from it with a little bundle of bunting at the end of one of them.

"We must find the King at once," said Gordon. He was terribly excited and angry. "It is easy enough to see what this means. They are going through the form of annexing this island to the other lands of the German government. They are robbing old Ollypybus of what is his. They have not even given him a silver watch for it."

The King was in his bungalow, facing the plaza. Messenwah was with him, and an equal number of each of their councils. The common danger had made them lie down together in peace; but they gave a murmur of relief as Gordon strode into the room with no ceremony, and greeted them with a curt wave of the hand.

"Now then, Stedman, be quick," he said. "Explain to them what this means; tell them that I will protect them; that I am anxious to see that Ollypybus is not cheated; that we will do all we can for them."

Outside, on the shore, a second boat's crew had landed a group of officers and a file of marines. They walked in all the dignity of full dress across the plaza to the flagpole, and formed in line on the three sides of it, with the marines facing the sea. The officers, from the captain with a prayer book in his hand, to the youngest middy, were as indifferent to the frightened natives about them as the other men had been. The natives, awed and afraid, crouched back among their huts, the marines and the sailors kept their eyes front, and the German captain opened his prayer-book. The debate in the bungalow was over.

"If you only had your uniform, sir," said Bradley, Sr., miserably.

"This is a little bit too serious for uniforms and bicycle medals," said Gordon. "And these men are used to gold lace."

He pushed his way through the natives, and stepped confidently across the plaza. The youngest middy saw him coming, and nudged the one next him with his elbow, and he nudged the next, but none of the officers moved, because the captain had begun to read.

"One minute, please," called Gordon.

He stepped out into the hollow square formed by the marines, and raised his helmet to the captain.

"Do you speak English or French?" Gordon said in French; "I do not understand German."

The captain lowered the book in his hands and gazed reflectively at Gordon through his spectacles, and made no reply.

"If I understand this," said the younger man, trying to be very impressive and polite, "you are laying claim to this land, in behalf of the German government."

The captain continued to observe him thoughtfully, and then said, "That iss so," and then asked, "Who are you?"

"I represent the King of this island, Ollypybus, whose people you see around you. I also represent the United States government that does not tolerate a foreign power near her coast, since the days of President Monroe and before. The treaty you have made with

Messenwah is an absurdity. There is only one king with whom to treat, and he—"

The captain turned to one of his officers and said something, and then, after giving another curious glance at Gordon, raised his book and continued reading, in a deep, unruffled monotone. The officer whispered an order, and two of the marines stepped out of line, and dropping the muzzles of their muskets, pushed Gordon back out of the enclosure, and left him there with his lips white, and trembling all over with indignation. He would have liked to have rushed back into the lines and broken the captain's spectacles over his suntanned nose and cheeks, but he was quite sure this would only result in his getting shot, or in his being made ridiculous before the natives, which was almost as bad; so he stood still for a moment, with his blood choking him, and then turned and walked back to where the King and Stedman were whispering together. Just as he turned, one of the men pulled the halyards, the ball of bunting ran up into the air, bobbed, twitched, and turned, and broke into the folds of the German flag. At the same moment the marines raised their muskets and fired a volley, and the officers saluted and the sailors cheered.

"Do you see that?" cried Stedman, catching Gordon's humor, to Ollypybus; "that means that you are no longer king, that strange people are coming here to take your land, and to turn your people into servants, and to drive you back into the mountains. Are you going to submit? are you going to let that flag stay where it is?"

Messenwah and Ollypybus gazed at one another with fearful, helpless eyes. "We are afraid," Ollypybus cried; "we do not know what we should do."

"What do they say?"

"They say they do not know what to do."

"I know what I'd do," cried Gordon. "If I were not an American consul, I'd pull down their old flag, and put a hole in their boat and sink her."

"Well, I'd wait until they get under way, before you do either of those things," said Stedman, soothingly. "That captain seems to be a man of much determination of character."

"But I will pull it down," cried Gordon. "I will resign, as Travis did. I am no longer consul. You can be consul if you want to. I promote you. I am going up a step higher. I mean to be king. Tell those two," he ran on excitedly, "that their only course and only hope is in me; that they must make me ruler of the island until this thing is over; that I will resign again as soon as it is settled, but that some one must act at once, and if they are afraid to, I am not, only they must give me authority to act for them. They must abdicate in my favor."

"Are you in earnest?" gasped Stedman.

"Don't I talk as if I were?" demanded Gordon, wiping the perspiration from his forehead.

"And can I be consul?" said Stedman, cheerfully.

"Of course. Tell them what I propose to do."

Stedman turned and spoke rapidly to the two kings. The people gathered closer to hear.

The two rival monarchs looked at one another in silence for a moment, and then both began to speak at once, their counsellors interrupting them and mumbling their guttural comments with anxious earnestness. It did not take them very long to see that they were all of one mind, and then they both turned to Gordon and dropped on one knee, and placed his hands on their foreheads, and Stedman raised his cap.

"They agree," he explained, for it was but pantomime to Albert. "They salute you as a ruler; they are calling you Tellaman, which means peacemaker. The Peacemaker, that is your title. I hope you will deserve it, but I think they might have chosen a more appropriate one."

"Then I'm really King?" demanded Albert, decidedly, "and I can do what I please? They give me full power. Quick, do they?"

"Yes, but don't do it," begged Stedman, "and just remember I am American consul now, and that is a much superior being to a crowned monarch; you said so yourself."

Albert did not reply to this, but ran across the plaza followed by the two Bradleys. The boats had gone.

"Hoist that flag beside the brass cannon," he cried, "and stand ready to salute it when I drop this one."

Bradley, Jr., grasped the halliards of the flag, which he had forgotten to raise and salute in the morning in all the excitement of the arrival of the man-of-war. Bradley, Sr., stood by the brass cannon, blowing gently on his lighted fuse. The Peacemaker took the halliards of the German flag in his two hands, gave a quick, sharp tug, and down came the red, white, and black piece of bunting, and the next moment young Bradley sent the stars and stripes up in their place. As it rose, Bradley's brass cannon barked merrily like a little bulldog, and the Peacemaker cheered.

"What don't you cheer, Stedman?" he shouted. "Tell those people to cheer for all they are worth. What sort of an American consul are you?"

Stedman raised his arm half-heartedly to give the time, and opened his mouth; but his arm remained fixed and his mouth open, while his eyes stared at the retreating boat of the German man-of-war. In the stern sheets of this boat, the stout German captain was struggling unsteadily to his feet; he raised his arm and waved it to some one on the great man-of-war, as though giving an order. The natives looked from Stedman to the boat, and even Gordon stopped in his cheering and stood motionless, watching. They had not very long to wait. There was a puff of white smoke, and a flash, and then a loud report, and across the water came a great black ball skipping lightly through and over the waves, as easily as a flat stone thrown by a boy. It seemed to come very slowly. At least it came slowly enough for every one to see that it was coming directly towards the brass cannon. The Bradleys certainly saw this, for they ran as fast as they could, and kept on running. The ball caught the cannon under its mouth, and tossed it in the air, knocking the flagpole into a dozen pieces, and passing on through two of the palm-covered huts.

"Great Heavens, Gordon!" cried Stedman; "they are firing on us."

But Gordon's face was radiant and wild.

"Firing on *us*!" he cried. "On *us*! Don't you see? Don't you understand? What do *we* amount to? They have fired on the American flag. Don't you see what that means? It means war. A great international war. And I am a war correspondent at last!" He ran up to Stedman and seized him by the arm so tightly that it hurt.

"By three o'clock," he said, "they will know in the office what has happened. The country will know it tomorrow when the paper is on the street; people will read it all over the world. The Emperor will hear of it at breakfast; the President will cable for further particulars. He will get them. It is the chance of a lifetime, and we are on the spot!"

Stedman did not hear this; he was watching the broadside of the ship to see another puff of white smoke, but there came no such sign. The two rowboats were raised, there was a cloud of black smoke from the funnel, a creaking of chains sounding faintly across the water, and the ship started at half speed and moved out of the harbor. The Opekians and the Hillmen fell on their knees, or to dancing, as best suited their sense of relief, but Gordon shook his head.

"They are only going to land the marines," he said; "perhaps they are going to the spot they stopped at before, or to take up another position further out at sea. They will land men and then shell the town, and the land forces will march here and cooperate with the vessel, and everybody will be taken prisoner or killed. We have the centre of the stage, and we are making history."

"I'd rather read it than make it," said Stedman. "You've got us in a senseless, silly position, Gordon, and a mighty unpleasant one. And for no reason that I can see, except to make copy for your paper."

"Tell those people to get their things together," said Gordon, "and march back out of danger into the woods. Tell Ollypybus I am going to fix things all right; I don't know just how yet, but I will, and now come after me as quickly as you can to the cable office. I've got to tell the paper all about it."

It was three o'clock before the "chap at Octavia" answered Stedman's signalling. Then Stedman delivered Gordon's message, and immediately shut off all connection, before the Octavia operator could question him. Gordon dictated his message in this way:—

"Begin with the date line, 'Opeki, June 22.'

"At seven o'clock this morning, the captain and officers of the German man-of-war, *Kaiser*, went through the ceremony of annexing this island in the name of the German Emperor, basing their right to do so on an agreement made with a leader of a wandering tribe, known as the Hillmen. King Ollypybus, the present monarch of Opeki, delegated his authority, as also did the leader of the Hillmen, to King Tallaman, or the Peacemaker, who tore down the German flag, and raised that of the United States in its place. At the same moment the flag was saluted by the battery. This salute, being mistaken for an attack on the *Kaiser*, was answered by that vessel. Her first shot took immediate effect, completely destroying the entire battery of the Opekians, cutting down the American flag, and destroying the houses of the people—"

"There was only one brass cannon and two huts," expostulated Stedman.

"Well, that was the whole battery, wasn't it?" asked Gordon, "and two huts is plural. I said houses of the people. I couldn't say two houses of the people. Just you send this as you get it. You are not an American consul at the present moment. You are an underpaid agent of a cable company, and you send my stuff as I write it. The American residents have taken refuge in the consulate—that's us," explained Gordon, "and the English residents have sought refuge in the woods—that's the Bradleys. King Tellaman—that's me—declares his intention of fighting against the annexation. The forces of the Opekians are under the command of Captain Thomas Bradley—I guess I might as well made him a colonel—of Colonel Thomas Bradley, of the English army.

"The American consul says—Now, what do you say, Stedman? Hurry up, please," asked Gordon, "and say something good and strong."

"You get me all mixed up," complained Stedman, plaintively. "Which am I now, a cable operator or the American consul?"

"Consul, of course. Say something patriotic and about your determination to protect the interests of your government, and all that." Gordon bit the end of his pencil impatiently, and waited.

"I won't do anything of the sort, Gordon," said Stedman; "you are getting me into an awful lot of trouble, and yourself too. I won't say a word."

"The American consul," read Gordon, as his pencil wriggled across the paper, "refuses to say anything for publication until he has communicated with the authorities at Washington, but from all I can learn he sympathizes entirely with Tellaman. Your correspondent has just returned from an audience with King Tellaman, who asks him to inform the American people that the Monroe doctrine will be sustained as long as he rules this island. I guess that's enough to begin with," said Gordon. "Now send that off quick, and then get away from the instrument before the man in Octavia begins to ask questions. I am going out to precipitate matters."

Gordon found the two kings sitting dejectedly side by side, and gazing grimly upon the disorder of the village, from which the people were taking their leave as quickly as they could get their few belongings piled upon the oxcarts. Gordon walked amongst them, helping them in every way he could, and tasting, in their subservience and gratitude, the sweets of sovereignty. When Stedman had locked up the cable office and rejoined him, he bade him tell Messenwah to send three of his youngest men and fastest runners back to the hills to watch for the German vessel and see where she was attempting to land her marines.

"This is a tremendous chance for descriptive writing, Stedman," said Gordon, enthusiastically, "all this confusion and excitement, and the people leaving their homes and all that. It's like the people getting out of Brussels before Waterloo, and then the scene at the foot of the mountains, while they are camping out there, until the Germans leave. I never had a chance like this before."

It was quite dark by six o'clock, and none of the three messengers had as yet returned. Gordon walked up and down the empty plaza and looked now at the horizon for the man-of-war, and again down the road back of the village. But neither the vessel nor the messengers, bearing word of her, appeared. The night passed without any incident, and in the morning Gordon's impatience became so great that he walked out to where the villagers were in camp and passed on half way up the mountain, but he could see no sign of the man-of-war. He came back more restless than before, and keenly disappointed.

"If something don't happen before three o'clock, Stedman," he said, "our second cablegram will have to consist of glittering generalities and a lengthy interview with King Tellaman, by himself."

Nothing did happen. Ollypybus and Messenwah began to breathe more freely. They believed the new king had succeeded in frightening the German vessel away forever. But the new king upset their hopes by telling them that the Germans had undoubtedly already landed, and had probably killed the three messengers.

"Now then," he said, with pleased expectation, as Stedman and he seated themselves in the cable office at three o'clock, "open it up and let's find out what sort of an impression we have made."

Stedman's face, as the answer came in to his first message of greeting, was one of strangely marked disapproval.

"What does he say?" demanded Gordon, anxiously.

"He hasn't done anything but swear yet," answered Stedman, grimly.

"What is he swearing about?"

"He wants to know why I left the cable yesterday. He says he has been trying to call me up for the last twenty-four hours ever since I sent my message at three o'clock The home office is jumping mad, and want me discharged. They won't do that, though," he said, in a cheerful aside, "because they haven't paid me my salary for the last eight months. He says—great Scott! this will please you, Gordon—he says that there have been over two hundred queries for matter from papers all over the United States, and from Europe. Your paper beat them on the news, and now the home office is packed with San Francisco reporters, and the telegrams are coming in every minute, and they have been abusing him for not answering them, and he says that I'm a fool. He wants as much as you can send, and all the details. He says all the papers will have to put 'By Yokohama Cable Company' on the top of each message they print, and that that is advertising the company, and is sending the stock up. It rose fifteen points on 'change in San Francisco today, and the president and the other officers are buying—"

"Oh, I don't want to hear about their old company," snapped out Gordon, pacing up and down in despair. "What am I to do? that's what I want to know. Here I have the whole country stirred up and begging for news. On their knees for it, and a cable all to myself and the only man on the spot, and nothing to say. I'd just like to know how long that German idiot intends to wait before he begins shelling this town and killing people. He has put me in a most absurd position."

"Here's a message for you, Gordon," said Stedman, with businesslike calm. "Albert Gordon, Correspondent," he read: "Try American consul. First message O.K.; beat the country; can take all you send. Give names of foreign residents massacred, and fuller account blowing up palace. Dodge."

The expression on Gordon's face as this message was slowly read off to him, had changed from one of gratified pride to one of puzzled consternation.

"What's he mean by foreign residents massacred, and blowing up of palace?" asked Stedman, looking over his shoulder anxiously. "Who is Dodge?"

"Dodge is the night editor," said Gordon, nervously. "They must have read my message wrong. You sent just what I gave you, didn't you?" he asked.

"Of course I did," said Stedman, indignantly.

"I didn't say anything about the massacre of anybody, did I?" asked Gordon. "I hope they are not improving on my account. What *am* I to do? This is getting awful. I'll have to go out and kill a few people myself. Oh, why don't that Dutch captain begin to do something! What sort of a fighter does he call himself? He wouldn't shoot at a school of porpoises. He's not—"

"Here comes a message to Leonard T. Travis, American consul, Opeki," read Stedman. "It's raining messages today. 'Send full details of massacre of American citizens by German sailors.' Secretary of—great Scott!" gasped Stedman, interrupting himself and gazing at his instrument with horrified fascination—"the Secretary of State."

"That settles it," roared Gordon, pulling at his hair and burying his face in his hands. "I have *got* to kill some of them now."

"Albert Gordon, Correspondent," read Stedman, impressively, like the voice of Fate. "Is Colonel Thomas Bradley commanding native forces at Opeki, Colonel Sir Thomas Kent-Bradley of Crimean war fame? Correspondent London *Times*, San Francisco Press Club."

"Go on, go on!" said Gordon, desperately. "I'm getting used to it now. Go on!"

"American consul, Opeki," read Stedman. "Home Secretary desires you to furnish list of names English residents killed during shelling of Opeki by ship of war *Kaiser*, and estimate of amount property destroyed. Stoughton, British Embassy, Washington."

"Stedman!" cried Gordon, jumping to his feet, "there's a mistake here somewhere. These people cannot all have made my message read like that. Some one has altered it, and now I have got to make these people here live up to that message, whether they like being massacred and blown up or not. Don't answer any of those messages, except the one from Dodge; tell him things have quieted down a bit, and that I'll send four thousand words on the flight of the natives from the village, and their encampment at the foot of the mountains, and of the exploring party we have sent out to look for the German vessel; and now I am going out to make something happen."

Gordon said that he would be gone for two hours at least, and as Stedman did not feel capable of receiving any more nerve-stirring messages, he cut off all connection with Octavia, by saying, "Good-by for two hours." and running away from the office. He sat down on a rock on the beach, and mopped his face with his handkerchief.

"After a man has taken nothing more exciting than weather reports from Octavia for a year," he soliloquized, "it's a bit disturbing to have all the crowned heads of Europe and their secretaries calling upon you for details of a massacre that never came off."

At the end of two hours Gordon returned from the consulate with a mass of manuscript in his hand.

"Here's three thousand words," he said desperately. "I never wrote more and said less in my life. It will make them weep at the office. I had to pretend that they knew all that had happened so far; they apparently do know more than we do, and I have filled it full of prophesies of more trouble ahead, and with interviews with myself and the two ex-Kings. The only news element in it is, that the messengers have returned to report that the German vessel is not in sight, and that there is no news. They think she has gone for good. Suppose she has, Stedman," he groaned, looking at him helplessly, "what *am* I going to do?"

"Well, as for me," said Stedman, "I'm afraid to go near that cable. It's like playing with a live wire. My nervous system won't stand many more such shocks as those they gave us this morning."

Gordon threw himself down dejectedly in a chair in the office, and Stedman approached his instrument gingerly, as though it might explode.

"He's swearing again," he explained sadly, in answer to Gordon's look of inquiry. "He wants to know when I am going to stop running away from the wire. He has a stack of messages to send, he says, but I guess he'd better wait and take your copy first; don't you think so?"

"Yes, I do," said Gordon. "I don't want any more messages than I've had. That's the best I can do," he said, as he threw his manuscript down beside Stedman. "And they can keep on cabling until the wire burns red hot, and they won't get any more."

There was silence in the office for some time, while Stedman looked over Gordon's copy, and Gordon stared dejectedly out at the ocean.

"This is pretty poor stuff, Gordon," said Stedman. "It's like giving people milk when they want brandy."

"Don't you suppose I know that?" growled Gordon. "It's the best I can do, isn't it? It's not my fault that we are not all dead now. I can't massacre foreign residents if there are no foreign residents, but I can commit suicide though, and I'll do it if something don't happen."

There was a long pause, in which the silence of the office was only broken by the sound of the waves beating on the coral reefs outside. Stedman raised his head wearily.

"He's swearing again," he said; "he says this stuff of yours is all nonsense. He says stock in the Y.C.C. has gone up to one hundred and two, and that owners are unloading and making their fortunes, and that this sort of descriptive writing is not what the company want."

"What's he think I'm here for?" cried Gordon. "Does he think I pulled down the German flag and risked my neck half a dozen times and had myself made King just to boom his Yokohama cable stock? Confound him! You might at least swear back. Tell him just what the situation is in a few words. Here, stop that rigmarole to the paper, and explain to your home office that we are awaiting developments, and that, in the meanwhile, they must put up with the best we can send them. Wait; send this to Octavia."

Gordon wrote rapidly, and read what he wrote as rapidly as it was written.

"Operator, Octavia. You seem to have misunderstood my first message. The facts in the case are these. A German man-of-war raised a flag on this island. It was pulled down and the American flag raised in its place and saluted by a brass cannon. The German man-of-war fired once at the flag and knocked it down, and then steamed away and has not been seen since. Two huts were upset, that is all the damage done; the battery consisted of the one brass cannon before mentioned. No one, either native or foreign, has been massacred. The English residents are two sailors. The American residents are the young man who is sending you this cable and myself. Our first message was quite true in substance, but perhaps misleading in detail. I made it so because I fully expected much more to happen immediately. Nothing has happened, or seems likely to happen, and that is the exact situation up to date. Albert Gordon."

"Now," he asked after a pause, "what does he say to that?"

"He doesn't say anything," said Stedman.

"I guess he has fainted. Here it comes," he added in the same breath. He bent toward his instrument, and Gordon raised himself from his chair and stood beside him as he read it off. The two young men hardly breathed in the intensity of their interest.

"Dear Stedman," he slowly read aloud. "You and your young friend are a couple of fools. If you had allowed me to send you the messages awaiting transmission here to you, you would not have sent me such a confession of guilt as you have just done. You had better leave Opeki at once or hide in the hills. I am afraid I have placed you in a somewhat compromising position with the company, which is unfortunate, especially as, if I am not mistaken, they owe you some back pay. You should have been wiser in your day, and bought Y.C.C. stock when it was down to five cents, as 'yours truly' did. You are not, Stedman, as bright a boy as some. And as for your friend, the war correspondent, he has queered himself for life. You see, my dear Stedman, after I had sent off your first message, and demands for further details came pouring in, and I could not get you at the wire to supply them, I took the liberty of sending some on myself."

"Great Heavens!" gasped Gordon.

Stedman grew very white under his tan, and the perspiration rolled on his cheeks.

"Your message was so general in its nature, that it allowed my imagination full play, and I sent on what I thought would please the papers, and, what was much more important to me, would advertise the Y.C.C. stock. This I have been doing while waiting for material from you. Not having a clear idea of the dimensions or population of Opeki, it is possible that I have done you and your newspaper friend some injustice. I killed off about a hundred American residents, two hundred English, because I do not like the English, and a hundred French. I blew up old Ollypybus and his palace with dynamite, and shelled the city, destroying some hundred thousand dollars' worth of property, and then I waited anxiously for your friend to substantiate what I had said. This he has most unkindly failed to do. I am very sorry, but much more so for him than for myself, for I, my dear friend, have cabled on to a man in San Francisco, who is one of the directors of the Y.C.C, to sell all my stock, which he has done at one hundred and two, and he is keeping the money until I come. And I leave Octavia this afternoon to reap my just reward. I am in about twenty thousand dollars on your little war, and I feel grateful. So much so that I will inform you that the ship of war *Kaiser* has arrived at San Francisco, for which port she sailed directly from Opeki. Her captain has explained the real situation, and offered to make every amend for the accidental indignity shown to our flag. He says he aimed at the cannon, which was trained on his vessel, and which had first fired on him. But you must know, my dear Stedman, that before his arrival, war vessels belonging to the several powers mentioned in my revised dispatches, had started for Opeki at full speed, to revenge the butchery of the foreign residents. A word, my dear young friend, to the wise is sufficient. I am indebted to you to the extent of twenty thousand dollars, and in return I give you this kindly advice. Leave Opeki. If there is no other way, swim. But leave Opeki."

The sun, that night, as it sank below the line where the clouds seemed to touch the sea, merged them both into a blazing, blood-red curtain, and colored the most wonderful spectacle that the natives of Opeki had ever seen. Six great ships of war, stretching out over a league of sea, stood blackly out against the red background, rolling and rising, and leaping forward, flinging back smoke and burning sparks up into the air behind them, and throbbing and panting like living creatures in their race for revenge. From the south, came a three-decked vessel, a great island of floating steel, with a flag as red as the angry sky behind it, snapping in the wind. To the south of it plunged two long low-lying torpedo boats, flying the French tri-color, and still further to the north towered three magnificent hulls of the White Squadron. Vengeance was written on every curve and line, on each straining engine rod, and on each polished gun muzzle.

And in front of these, a clumsy fishing boat rose and fell on each passing wave. Two sailors sat in the stern, holding the rope and tiller, and in the bow, with their backs turned forever toward Opeki, stood two young boys, their faces lit by the glow of the setting sun and stirred by the sight of the great engines of war plunging past them on their errand of vengeance.

"Stedman," said the elder boy, in an awestruck whisper, and with a wave of his hand, "we have not lived in vain."

www.ingramcontent.com/pod-product-compliance
Lightning Source LLC
Chambersburg PA
CBHW020150180626
46810CB00004B/1823